FREDDY'S COUSIN

WEEDLY

The Complete FREDDY THE PIG Series
Available or Coming Soon from The Overlook Press

FREDDY'S
Cousin
WEEDLY

BY

WALTER R. BROOKS

Illustrated by

KURT WIESE

THE OVERLOOK PRESS
WOODSTOCK & NEW YORK

If you enjoyed this book, very likely you will be interested not only in the other Freddy books published in this series, but also in joining the *Friends of Freddy,* an organization of Freddy devotees.

We will be pleased to hear from any reader about our "Freddy" publishing program. You can easily contact us by logging on the either THE OVERLOOK PRESS website, or the Freddy website.

The website addresses are as follows:
THE OVERLOOK PRESS:
www.overlookpress.com

FREDDY:
www.friendsoffreddy.org

We look forward to hearing from you soon.

First published in the United States in 2002 by
The Overlook Press, Peter Mayer Publishers, Inc.
Woodstock & New York

WOODSTOCK:
One Overlook Drive
Woodstock, NY 12498
www.overlookpress.com
[for individual orders, bulk and special sales, contact our Woodstock office]

NEW YORK:
141 Wooster Street
New York, NY 10012

∞ The paper used in this book meets the requirements for paper permanence as described in the ANSI Z39.48-1992 standard.

Dust jacket and endpaper artwork courtesy of the Lee Secrest collection and archive.

Cataloging-in-Publication Data is available from the Library of Congress

Brooks, Walter R., 1886-1958.
Freddy's cousin Weedly / Walter R. Brooks ; illustrated by Kurt Wiese.
p. cm.

Manufactured in the United States of America
ISBN 1-58567-309-9
1 3 5 7 9 8 6 4 2

ILLUSTRATIONS

☼

ILLUSTRATIONS

FREDDY'S COUSIN

WEEDLY

Chapter 1

Jinx, the cat, sat on the bank of the little brook that runs through the Bean farm. He had just had his supper and he was waiting for Freddy, the pig. Freddy was late. Jinx just sat and waved his tail slowly. Then he waved it faster. He had an idea it made the time pass more quickly when he waved it fast. He tried it both ways several times, but there wasn't really any way to tell, so he curled his tail around him and washed his face.

He washed his face and his paws and his

stomach, and then he tried to wash his back between the shoulders. He tried every way to reach it. He could twist his head around and see a little dusty patch of fur between his shoulders, but he couldn't quite reach it with his tongue. Finally, he twisted around so far that he fell right over.

He got up and started to try again and then he stopped suddenly and looked very hard at a daisy that seemed to be leaning over a clump of grass and looking down at him. He had an idea the daisy had laughed. But when he looked at it, it only nodded and looked back at him with the blank and rather foolish expression that daisies have.

Jinx walked up and down the bank for a while. "Where *is* that pig?" he said. "I suppose he's at his poetry again, and has forgotten all about the time. Deliver me from a poet!"

He sighed and sat down again and looked at the water, and wondered about it. It came down through the woods, and ran along beside them for a way, and then it cut down through a pasture and into the duck pond at one end and out of it at the other. And then it curved around, past the farm buildings, and ducked under a little bridge and went out into the wide world. Here it was fairly deep, and Jinx leaned over and tried to see what was on the bottom, but he could only see the reflection of his own face. However, that was not unpleasant to look at. "Not at all," said Jinx to himself. "Quite the contrary. You'd have to go a long way to match that face, just for sheer downright good looks." And he tried on some of his best expressions.

He was just trying to look like a combination of George Washington and Julius Caesar when he thought he saw two little shadows moving through the water. He looked more closely and made out two minnows, who were staring up at him. They grinned and waggled their fins derisively, and he thought that one of them put out his tongue.

It isn't any fun being caught doing something foolish, even by a minnow, and Jinx got mad. "You better quit that," he said angrily, "or I'll make you laugh out of the other side of your mouths."

Of course the fish couldn't hear him, but

they could see that he was mad. They swam up closer and looked at him, and then they looked at each other, and if you ever saw a minnow giggle, these minnows did. That enraged Jinx even more. He lashed his tail for a second and then he pounced on them. At least he thought it was going to be a pounce, but he had forgotten about the water, and it turned out to be a splash. The minnows, with a flick of their tails, were off downstream, and Jinx, who didn't like water any better than most cats do, crawled out, spluttering. And there was Freddy.

"Well, well," said the pig. "I didn't know you went in for fancy diving, Jinx. What do they call that one? I must try it."

"Don't be funny," said Jinx crossly. He shook himself and sprinkled Freddy generously with water. But the pig didn't mind. "Fine," he said. "Very refreshing. Do it again, will you?"

"Where have you been?" asked Jinx. "I've been waiting here, hours."

"I'm sorry," said Freddy, "but just as I was starting, some people came to call on Mr. and

Mrs. Bean, and I waited around to find out who they were."

"What difference does it make?" said Jinx. "They can't call on the Beans when the Beans have gone to Europe for the summer."

"That's just it," said the pig. "They came in a car and brought a lot of trunks and things. I guess they planned to come and stay a month or two. But when they found the Beans were away for the summer they got in a window and opened the house, and then they just unpacked and moved in."

"For Pete's sake!" said the cat. "They can't do that. And how'd they find out about the Beans? You didn't talk to them, did you?" For it is a rule among animals never to talk to strange humans, and indeed most animals never talk even to the people that own them. It had been a good many years before Mr. Bean, who was certainly as kind and friendly to his animals as any farmer in New York State, had found out that his animals could talk.

"Of course I didn't," said Freddy. "Mr. Witherspoon came by, and they went out and asked him. I tried to listen, but the woman shooed me away." He thought a minute. "I didn't like her much," he said.

"We ought to do something about it," said Jinx. "How many of them are there?"

"Just two. The man is little and has on a sort of cowboy hat, and the woman is tall and thin and looks like this." He tried to purse up his lips to look very prim and severe, but a pig's face isn't built to look that way and the expression wasn't a success. "I didn't like either of them much, but I didn't like the woman most."

"H'm," said Jinx thoughtfully. "Well, of course, maybe they're all right, and even if they aren't—" He stopped, and then he said: "I tell you what we'd better do. When we get back from your cousin's, send word to your friend the sheriff. He can come out to the farm and talk to them, and if there's anything queer about them, he will send them away."

Freddy agreed that that was the sensible thing to do, and they started up along the brook. They went through the woods and up over the hill and down the other side to the

Macy farm where Freddy's cousin, Ernest, lived. Freddy hadn't seen Ernest for over a year. He would probably have gone to see him oftener, but Ernest always fell asleep when Freddy read him his poetry. Not that that was anything against the poetry. Ernest was always falling asleep. Freddy said that he fell asleep a lot oftener than he woke up. Of course, if you think about that you see that it couldn't be so. But it is one of those things that poets say that don't really make sense, and yet you know just what they mean. For Ernest was probably the sleepiest pig that ever lived.

But anyway, Freddy had decided that he ought to go call on him, and meet his wife and children, and Jinx, who liked children, whether they were pig children or human children, had said he would go along.

So the cat and the pig walked down the hill into the Macy barnyard and knocked at the pigpen door.

After a minute, a face appeared at the window. "Yes?" it said.

"Hello," said Freddy. "Aren't you Cousin Cora?"

"Why goodness me!" said the face. "It must be Cousin Frederick. Come right in." And she flung the door open. "Ernest! Ernest! Wake up. It's your Cousin Frederick come all the way over from Beans' to visit you. Well, well, Cousin Frederick, you're quite a stranger. Ernest has been wondering what had become of you. We don't see much company here, you know. You ought to come oftener."

"I know, I know," said Freddy. "I should have come before, but you know how it is. So much going on."

There was the sound of a hearty yawn from the other room and after a minute Ernest came in. "Ho, ho, hum!" he yawned. "Hello, Cousin. Ho, hi, *yaw!* Must excuse me, I was up late last night; didn't get to bed till nearly seven, and I slept a little late this morning."

"Morning!" said Freddy. "It's nearly seven in the evening now."

"Is it?" said Ernest. "Well, who'd have thought it? I don't really feel that I've had my sleep out. Cora, where are the—ho, *hooo!*— where are the children?"

"Come out and shake hands with your cousin Frederick."

So Cora called the children, and they came in and were introduced. Ernest, Jr., looked and acted a good deal like his father, for he was very plump, and kept rubbing his eyes sleepily. But the second son was a very small and timid little pig who refused to say "How do you do," but hid behind his father and peeked out. All they could see of him was one pink ear and one small bright eye. His name was William, but everybody called him *Little Weedly*.

"Come, come, Weedly," said Cora. "Come out and shake hands with your Cousin Frederick."

But Freddy said: "Let him alone, Cora. He'll come out when he gets ready."

"I'm sure I don't know what to do about this shyness of his," said Cora. "My Aunt Hattie was the same way; she couldn't even say 'Good morning' to the family without blushing. And my sister,—my goodness, Ernest, you remember how she fainted away when you were introduced to her for the first time?"

"Well," said Freddy with a laugh, "I suppose it was kind of a shock meeting Ernest for the first time. —Oh, goodness; he's gone to sleep again. Hey, Ernest, wake up."

Ernest opened his eyes. "Dear, dear," he said, "I'm afraid I dropped off. What were you saying?"

"We were just saying," said Freddy, "that nobody ever knew whether you were shy or not because you never stayed awake long enough for anyone to find out."

"Something in it," said Ernest with a laugh. "Yes— Oh, ho, hi, *yaw*—something in it. Yes." And he closed his eyes again.

"There he goes," said Cora. "Well, Cousin Frederick, I wish you and your friend Jinx would give me your advice about Little Weedly. How can we get him over his being so scary of everything?"

Well, they talked about it for a while. Freddy suggested sending him away to school, but of course there aren't any preparatory schools for pigs nowadays; and then he suggested spanking him, but they all decided it wouldn't be fair to spank him for something he couldn't help.

"And what is your advice, Mr. Jinx?" said Cora.

"Well," said Jinx, "from what you say I judge he doesn't see much of anybody here but the family. He ought to be around with a lot of other animals all the time. Send him out into the world: that'll make a pig of him."

"But he's such a little fellow to go away all by himself," said Cora.

"Napoleon was a little fellow, and look where he got to," said Jinx, trying to look as much like Napoleon as possible.

"And where would we send him?" Cora went on. "Cousin Frederick, if you could just take him over to the Bean farm with you for a while—"

"Dear me," said Freddy hastily, "I wish I could. But I really wouldn't have time to look after him. There's so much to do while the Beans are away, and then you know I'm president of the First Animal Bank now."

"Oh, yes," said Cora. "I've heard about your bank for animals. It sounds fine. Is it—" She stopped. Little Weedly had whispered something in her ear. "What is it?" she said.

Then she laughed, and turned to Jinx. "He says he thinks you're beautiful. He says he wishes he could grow up to be like you."

"Well, well," said Jinx, smiling self-consciously, "so you'd like to grow up to look like me, young man, would you?" But Little Weedly had disappeared behind his mother again. "Smart young fellow," Jinx said. "Why not take him along, Freddy? He's got good stuff in him, that little pig."

But Freddy said no, he was sorry but it was out of the question.

"Well, I'll take him, ma'am, if you'll trust him with me," said Jinx. "I haven't got the education Freddy has, but there's a few things I can teach him. Eh, Weedly? Come over here and sit by your Uncle Jinx." And to everybody's surprise, Little Weedly came out from behind his mother and sat down beside the cat.

They talked for a little while longer and then they got up to go, for Little Weedly was afraid of the dark, and the sun had already gone down. Little Weedly kissed his mother goodby, and then he kissed his father. Ernest had gone to sleep again, but he opened one eye and said: "Eh, Weedly? Ho, hum. Tell me when breakfast is ready," and shut the eye again.

"Well, Mr. Jinx," said Cora, "I can't tell you how grateful I am to you. I hope he won't be too much trouble. If he is, you send him right home."

But Jinx assured her that he would be no trouble at all, and after saying goodby, the three animals set out for the Bean farm, Weedly trotting along contentedly beside his new uncle.

Chapter 2

Jinx usually lived in the farmhouse kitchen, but of course with the Beans away in Europe, there was nobody to open the door and let him in and out, so he had moved down into the barn for the summer. When he got home, he fixed up a bed for Little Weedly in the box stall, and then, while Freddy went down to Centerboro to see the sheriff, he wandered over toward the house to see what he could find out about the newcomers.

The house was shut up tight, but there was a light in the parlor window. Jinx mewed at the door to get in, and then he jumped up on the sill and mewed at the window. He could see a tall bony woman sitting at the table drinking a cup of tea. She had a black silk shawl around her shoulders and a funny old-fashioned bonnet on her head, and when she lifted the teacup she held her little finger out straight. Jinx had used his saddest and most mournful mew. It made you think of little children crying and cats dying of starvation and all sorts of sorrowful things, and you would be pretty hard-hearted if you could keep from going to the door. But the woman didn't even look up. So Jinx made the mew even more heart-rending until you would think that he had the most awful stomach-ache that any cat ever had.

And at last the woman got up. She came and opened the window and said: "Scat! Stop that caterwauling before I take the broom-stick to you."

So Jinx jumped down. He was pretty mad. "Keep me out of my own house, will you?" he said. "Well, we'll see about this." He went around to the front door. Standing on his hind legs, he was just able to reach the bell. He put his paw on it and kept it on until he heard footsteps. Then he stepped to one side as the door opened.

A little man with a bald head opened the door wide. "Good evening, sir or madam, as the case may be," he said, bowing very low. Then he straightened up. "Eh!" he said in surprise. "Not a soul here! Dearie me and welladay, not a single, solitary soul." He walked out and looked around and Jinx slipped inside.

The woman had her back to Jinx when he came into the parlor, and he went under the sofa. In a minute the man came in.

"Well now, there's a funny thing, Effie," he said. "Doorbell rings and nobody there, nobody, not anybody at all. What a thing, eh? Eh? That was queer, wasn't it?"

"You talk too much, Snedeker," she said. "It was probably just neighborhood boys, playing tricks. Just let me catch them once, and there'll be no more of that." And she crooked her little finger genteelly as she took a small sip of tea.

"Eh, eh, all very well," said the man. "But there's no neighborhood around here. Can't be neighborhood boys if there isn't any neighborhood. Eh, Effie?"

"Where there's people, there's a neighborhood," said the woman, "and where there's a neighborhood, there's boys, and where there's boys, there's mischief. Don't bother your head about them, but go do as I told you to." But whatever it was she had told him to do, Jinx didn't find out, for at that minute the doorbell rang again.

"You stay here, Snedeker," said the woman, getting up. "I'll see to it this time." She took a broom from the corner and went as quietly as she could out through the back door. After a minute of silence there was a loud *thwack*! and a yell, and then a sound of excited voices and the front door opened and in came the woman, followed by a tall man with long drooping moustaches and a silver star pinned to his vest.

"Well, ma'am," said the tall man, "to hit

—there was a loud thwack!

the sheriff of this county with a broom when in pursuance of his duty ain't no way to prove to him that you're law-abiding citizens. These here premises belong to Mr. Bean, and what I want to know is: why do I find you occupying said premises, and what's to hinder my chargin' you with unlawfully entering same, and takin' you down to the Centerboro jail?"

The sheriff didn't always talk this way, but he knew that the language of the law is pretty terrifying to most people, and so he used it when he wanted to impress anybody. Besides, he had just been hit behind with a broom.

"Why, sheriff," said the woman, with a sour smile, "that was a bad mistake on my part, and I admit it freely. But some boys have been ringing the doorbell tonight, and then running off, and when you rang I thought it was them again. I'm very sorry, and won't you have a cup of tea?"

"One thing at a time," said the sheriff. "Are you occupyin' these premises with Mr. Bean's knowledge and consent?"

"Why, I'm Mr. Bean's Aunt Effie—Mrs. Snedeker. We've come all the way from Orenville, Ohio, to pay the Beans a visit. We didn't know they were away. But now we're here— well, we'd made all our arrangements to be away, and so we thought we might as well stay a while. Snedeker, show the sheriff William's letter."

Mr. Snedeker began feeling in all his pockets. From one he pulled out a ball of string and a pipe and a small bottle of cough medicine and a candle end, and from another he produced a driver's license and some matches and a china duck and two lollipops, and from a third two watches and a screw driver and—

"Come, come, Snedeker," said Aunt Effie, "the sheriff doesn't want to decorate a Christmas tree; he wants to see the letter."

"Got it somewhere," said Mr. Snedeker, beginning on another pocket. "Eh, Effie, here's that darning egg you were looking for last week. That's funny, eh? And a picture of Niagara Falls— Eh, here it is, here it is." And he handed the sheriff a letter.

"It's Mr. Bean's handwriting, all right," said the sheriff. " 'My dear aunt,' " he read.

" 'I hope this finds you as it leaves me, in good health and spirits.' H'm, he spelt 'spirits' wrong, but I guess that's no harm. H'm, h'm. 'If you pass by this way going to Albany, we will be glad to have you stop for dinner.' Well now, ma'am," said the sheriff, "that ain't exactly an invitation to come for a long visit."

"Oh, you know how William is," said Aunt Effie. "He never says more than a quarter of what he means. Why look how he signs the letter. Anybody else would sign: 'Your affectionate nephew.' But he just signs: 'Respectfully, William Bean.' "

"Yes, that's true," said the sheriff. "What's the meaning of this postscript—something about a silver teapot—"

"Oh, nothing," said Aunt Effie, picking the letter quickly out of the sheriff's hand. "Just some family business."

"Well, it seems to be all in order," said the sheriff. "You understand, ma'am, it was my duty to investigate."

"Certainly, sheriff, certainly. And now won't you have a cup of tea?"

"Afraid I must be getting back," the sheriff

replied. "I just remembered I left the jail locked."

"Left it locked!" said Mr. Snedeker. "Well, that's all right, ain't it, eh? Prisoners can't get out."

"They can't get *in*," said the sheriff. "Most of 'em are out visiting their families tonight or at the movies, and they're going to be good and sore if they come back and find they can't get in."

"Sounds like a pretty nice jail," said Aunt Effie.

"It *is* a nice jail, if I do say so," said the sheriff. "One of the most popular jails in the state. I have to make it nice, or I wouldn't have any job. You see, ma'am, we don't have any crime in Centerboro, and if I didn't keep a nice comfortable jail that people want to stay in, why I wouldn't get any prisoners to look after, and where'd my job be? So I got the cells all fixed up with good beds, and we got a game room and tennis courts and so on, and we set a better table than the hotel does. Folks like to stay in my jail, so now and then they break a few unimportant laws so they can get sent there. I don't say it's right of 'em, but it's reasonable."

"Well, I'm glad there's no crime in Centerboro," said Aunt Effie, "but how about these boys that were ringing the doorbell just now?"

"There aren't any boys around here, ma'am," said the sheriff. "My guess is, it was some of the animals on this farm. I expect you've heard about Mr. Bean's animals?"

"I've read about them in the papers," said Aunt Effie. "Smart enough animals, I suppose, but that's one reason we thought we'd stay here for a while. I can't understand William going away and leaving them all alone here. We are going to stay and look after them."

"Well, I don't know," said the sheriff. "Mr. Bean knew what he was doing all right, when he left them to run the place. I guess you haven't talked to any of 'em yet, have you, ma'am?"

"Talked to 'em, eh?" said Mr. Snedeker with a giggle. "That's a good one, that is." And Aunt Effie said: "Do I look like the kind of woman who'd go around talking to animals? Oh, I know," she said: "there was a lot in the newspapers about how they can talk and about how they had the first animal bank in the country, and so on. Folderol and fiddle-sticks! Don't you try to fill us up with that kind of nonsense, sheriff."

"I can't make you believe it if you don't want to," said the sheriff. "But if I were you—"

"If I were *you*, sheriff," interrupted Aunt Effie, "I'd stop talking foolishness."

"Have it your own way," said the sheriff stiffly. "But if you want to stay here, you'd better make friends with them—that's all I have to say. Good evening, ma'am. And to you, sir." And he went out.

"Eh, well, suppose there's something in it, Effie?" said Mr. Snedeker. "Animals talking? Could be, you know. Parrots talk—why not animals? Eh, Effie?"

"Well, there's one thing certain," said his wife, "nobody ever said *you* couldn't talk, Snedeker. Why don't you go up in the attic and look for that teapot?"

"I will, Effie, I will. Only I'd like to ask you

if you meant what you said to the sheriff about staying here for a while, eh? I thought you said we'd start back to Orenville as soon as you got the teapot."

"And so we will. But it may take some time to find it. You may be sure William has got it hidden away in a safe place. And while we're staying here, we're going to see that this farm is properly run. It's a sin and a shame for them to go off and leave everything to rack and ruin. Leaving the animals to run the place, indeed! I never heard such nonsense!"

Jinx, who had been listening all the time under the couch, was doing some hard thinking. He knew something about that silver teapot. Mrs. Bean prized it very highly and only used it on special occasions, and once when she had been polishing it with one of Mr. Bean's old flannel nightcaps, which she saved for that purpose, he had heard her tell Mr. Bean that she would have felt pretty badly if he had given the teapot to his Aunt Effie.

"Couldn't give it to her," Mr. Bean had said. " 'Twasn't mine to give. My grandmother gave it to me, and told me to keep it for my wife."

"Which you did, Mr. B," said Mrs. Bean. "And yet I feel sort of sorry for her, too, not having it. She wanted it so much, and she does so love tea parties."

"Tea parties, tea parties!" Mr. Bean grumbled. "Seemingly that's all they do out in Ohio is give tea parties."

"No harm in that," said Mrs. Bean. "I expect we'd give 'em too if we had anybody to give 'em to." She held the teapot up so that it glittered in the sunlight that came through the kitchen window. "It's a pretty piece of silver. And yet, you know, if she'd asked us nicely for it, instead of acting as if we'd stolen it from her, I'm not sure I wouldn't have given it to her. I suppose you'll say I'm too soft-hearted."

"No harm in that either," said Mr. Bean gruffly, and patted her on the shoulder as he went out toward the barn. But in a minute he came back and poked his head in the door. "As long as you don't give way to it," he said, with the little grumble that was what he used for a laugh. And Mrs. Bean laughed too and put the teapot away.

So Jinx knew that the Snedekers must not be allowed to get that teapot. He also knew where it was, for he had been with Mrs. Bean when, before she left for Europe, she had wrapped it in a flannel petticoat and put it in the bottom of an old horsehide trunk in the attic.

He slipped out from under the couch and ran upstairs. But the attic door was closed. He thought a minute and then went into the spare bedroom. "Hey! Webb!" he said in a cautious whisper. And in about half a minute he felt a tickling on his left ear and a tiny voice said: "Hi, Jinx! What's on your mind?"

Mr. Webb was a spider who usually lived out in the cowbarn. But before the Beans had gone away, Mrs. Bean had been worried about flies getting into the house, and especially into the spare bedroom, so Mr. and Mrs. Webb had moved in there and had built their fly traps in every corner of the room. As a matter of fact, no flies had come in, and the Webbs couldn't catch enough of them to make a living. But they kept on living there just the same because they knew it would please Mrs. Bean, and Mr. Webb went down to the cowbarn every day, just as a man would go to his office, and caught enough flies to keep them going. This was really pretty nice of Mr. Webb, for though you or I could have gone from the house to the cowbarn in a couple of minutes, it was a long weary tramp for a spider, particularly at the end of the day when he was tired out hunting.

"Careful, Webb," said Jinx. "Don't get on my nose and make me sneeze, or those people will hear me. Have they been up here?"

"Turning the house upside down ever since they got here," said Mr. Webb. "I heard the woman say she was Mr. Bean's aunt. She doesn't look like him."

"How can you tell whether she does or not?" said Jinx. "With all those whiskers."

"Whiskers?" said Mr. Webb. "I didn't notice she had whiskers."

"I mean Mr. Bean's whiskers," said the cat. "He's got so many that nobody has ever seen what he really looks like, so how would you know whether his aunt looked like him or not? But anyway," he said, "we've got to do something about it." And he explained.

Mr. Webb didn't say anything for a time. He paced up and down between Jinx's ears, deep in thought. At last he said: "If we can keep them from finding the teapot tonight before they go to bed, then before morning we can get word to the other animals, and they'll have to do something. But in the meantime, we've got to keep Uncle Snedeker from finding it if he goes up in the attic. Listen; that sounds like him coming now. You follow him up if you can, and try to scare him. There's a crack over the window where Mrs. Webb and I can get up there. We'll do what we can. So long; I'd better hurry."

Jinx could hear feet coming up the stairs. In a minute he saw Uncle Snedeker, with a candle in his hand, walk along the hall and open the door to the attic stairs. Jinx followed him and when Uncle Snedeker held up the candle to look around, the cat darted behind an old chest of drawers.

Mrs. Bean was a good housekeeper. Everything in the attic was piled up and packed away neatly. The floor was swept, and there were even clean little muslin curtains at the windows. "Neat as a new pin," said Uncle Snedeker. "Let's see, now, Snedeker; where'll you begin, eh? Where'll you start? That big chest in the corner looks like a likely place to find a silver teapot in, eh? Well, then— Whoosh!" he said suddenly, and began pawing at his face with both stands. "Spiders! Ugh, how I hate the nasty things!" For Mr. Webb had dropped from a rafter on to Uncle Snedeker's nose, and had run down across his face and then jumped to the floor.

Uncle Snedeker brushed himself off, and then he picked up the candle and looked around, but didn't see anything. If he had looked up, he would have seen Mrs. Webb, but he didn't. He was just starting for the big chest when Mrs. Webb jumped.

Uncle Snedeker was pretty bald, and Mrs. Webb landed on the top of his head and skidded halfway down his forehead before her feet took hold properly. She ran down his face and jumped just as Mr. Webb had done. Then she and her husband climbed back on to the rafter, all ready for another jump, if it should be necessary.

But it wasn't necessary. For Uncle Snedeker was still saying "Whoosh!" and "Phow!" and all the other things people say when bugs drop on them, when Jinx gave a low ghostly moan. Uncle Snedeker dropped his candle and bolted down the stairs and slammed the door at the foot of them behind him.

Well, they had saved the teapot for the time being, but Jinx was certainly worse off than he had been before, for he was shut in the attic with no way to get out. Of course he could sit down and howl, and if he howled long enough, somebody would come and let him out. But he had an idea it would probably be Aunt Effie who would come, and Aunt Effie was entirely too handy with a broom.

He talked it over with the Webbs, but they couldn't think of anything. "I tell you what I'll do though, Jinx," said Mr. Webb. "I'll go on down to the pigpen and tell Freddy.

Maybe he can organize a rescue party."

But Jinx said no. There was a heavy dew that night, and although it was nothing that would have bothered you or me, a spider would be certain to step into a dozen puddles that were over his ankles. And Mr. Webb was subject to colds. He had had one cold after another all that spring.

Mrs. Webb was much relieved. "I'd rather Webb didn't go, and that's the truth," she said. "He feels so bad when he has a cold, and then he sneezes all the time, and the flies hear him and get away. You know yourself, Jinx, it's no use going out hunting if you're sneezing every two seconds. It got so the flies just laughed at him. They sat in rows on the wall and waited for him to sneeze and they laughed their heads off. They even invited their friends to come hear the sneezing spider. You can't imagine how trying it was."

"Jinx doesn't want to hear about our troubles, Mother," said Mr. Webb. "Besides, that's all over now."

"I just wanted him to understand why I thought you oughtn't to go," said Mrs. Webb.

"But goodness, I'll go down and tell Freddy myself. A breath of air'll do me good."

But Jinx wouldn't hear of it. "No indeed, ma'am," he said. "I certainly won't let a lady do a thing I can't do myself. No, no; I'll just curl up here on this old mattress and Webb can see Freddy in the morning." And so they left it at that.

Chapter 3

Jinx had forgotten all about Little Weedly, whom he had left curled up on an old blanket in the box stall of the barn. But Little Weedly hadn't forgotten Jinx. He lay there staring into the darkness and wondering why his handsome new uncle didn't come back. For Jinx had said he'd only be a few minutes. "Oh dear, oh dear!" said Little Weedly to himself. "Why *doesn't* he come?" And like all scary people, he began trying to scare himself worse, by thinking of all the terrible things that could have happened to Jinx, until he was in a regular panic.

In the stall next door he could.hear Hank, the old white horse, breathing in long slow breaths, and occasionally muttering in his sleep. You can't imagine anything much more peaceful to listen to. But if you want to scare yourself there are always, in any old building, creaks and snaps and rustlings that you can imagine are bears or burglars or bugaboos of unprecedented ferocity, just crawling up on you and waiting to pounce. And so by the time there did come a sound that he really couldn't explain, Weedly was almost ready to fly into a fit.

It wasn't a very large sound. In fact, if you or I had been lying awake and had heard it, we would merely have said: "H'm, mouse somewhere," and would have turned over and tried to go to sleep. And we would have been right, too, for it was a mouse named Quik, who was sitting on the edge of the manger just over Weedly's head, eating a peanut.

Quik and his three brothers, Eek and Eeny

and Cousin Augustus, had gone to bed at their regular time, up in the hay mow. Usually they lived in the house, but while the Beans were away there weren't any crumbs under the dining room table, or any little saucers of things that Mrs. Bean left out for them, so they had moved down into the barn. The other three mice had gone right to sleep, but Quik had been wakeful, probably because he had eaten a coffee bean at dinner, and at last he had got up. He crawled out of the hay and walked up the wall to a hole under the eaves, and out on to the roof. But an owl hooted and he went back in again. All of the owls in the neighborhood were friends of his, but it is hard to recognize friends in the dark, and if there was a mistake it would be too late to ex-plain who he was after he was eaten. So he went back in and foraged around in the part of the barn where the boys used to play when they were home. For where there are boys, there are usually crumbs. And sure enough, he found an old peanut.

Quik took the peanut into the box stall and climbed up on the manger and started to eat it. It was so dark he didn't see Weedly at all. The peanut was pretty stale, but Quik didn't get peanuts very often and I'm afraid he smacked his lips a good deal as he munched it, although mice, as a general rule, have very good manners. It was this smacking that Weedly heard. He began to tremble, and that made a rustling noise. Quik looked down and saw something white on the floor that moved a little bit, and that startled him so that he dropped his peanut, which hit Little Weedly on the nose. And then Little Weedly lost all control of himself, and began to squeal "Help! Mamma! Help!" at the top of his lungs, and he ran, still squealing, out into the barnyard.

For his size, a pig can squeal louder than almost any other animal. Little Weedly was small but in five seconds every animal on the Bean farm was tumbling out of bed, shouting: "Hey! What's wrong? What's the matter?" Quik, who had, of course, been nearest the first squeal, fainted dead away and didn't come to until all the excitement was over. Hank woke up with a snort, and came clumping out, and Robert and Georgie, the two dogs, rushed out, and the three cows, Mrs. Wiggins and Mrs. Wurzburger and Mrs. Wogus, pushed aside the little lace curtains at their windows in the cowbarn and stuck their broad noses out. Freddy came out of the pigpen, and the ducks, Alice and Emma, came waddling up from the pond as fast as their short legs could carry them, and the chickens, clucking and cackling, piled out of the henhouse, Henrietta in the lead, and Charles, the rooster, as usual, talking very loud, but bringing up the rear.

When Little Weedly came out of the barn door, he headed straight for home. He dodged through the animals that were gathering in the barnyard, and galloped up across the brook and into the woods, yelling all the time. He was afraid of the dark night, and of the woods, but he was more afraid of that box stall where he had had the terrible experience of having a peanut drop on his nose out of nowhere. And if he had got home, this story wouldn't have had much more to say about him. He would have gone down in history just as a terribly bashful pig, and that would be the end of him.

But up in the woods the squealing had been heard, too. Birds stirred on the branches, and rabbits and chipmunks and squirrels came to their doorways and sniffed and pricked up their ears. And Peter, the bear, who had been curled up in the raspberry patch, where he had been sleeping lately so that he could keep an eye on the blue jays who came early in the morning to steal his berries, got up and came sleepily out to see what was going on. And he came out right in the middle of the path up which Little Weedly was galloping.

Bears are good-natured animals. They aren't any more ferocious than mice; they're just bigger. Down the path Peter could just make out that something was coming, and he stood up on his hind legs to see better. Weedly came tearing along toward him, screeching like a fire engine, but just before he got to the bear he stumbled over a projecting root and fell flat.

"Hello there," said Peter. "You must be

. . . he tore back down the path.

the little pig that says 'Wee, wee' all the way home. What's all the trouble?''

Weedly looked up and saw towering over him, a great shaggy animal, such as he had never seen before. Peter held out a big paw to help him up, but Weedly thought the creature was trying to catch him. He jumped up and tore back down the path the way he had come, squealing just as loud as he had before. Only now he was calling on his Uncle Jinx for help, instead of his mother.

"Well, my goodness!" said Peter, and went back to the raspberry patch.

In the Bean barnyard, the animals had gathered around Freddy, who was telling them about Little Weedly. "Jinx said he'd look after him," said the pig, "but evidently Jinx has gone off hunting somewhere, and he got scared. Do you know what scared him, Hank?"

"Didn't know anything about it till he began squealing," said the horse. "My land, he scared *me* out of a year's growth. He ain't coming back, is he, Freddy?"

"He didn't sound as if he intended to," said

the pig. "No, he's gone back home, and I don't believe—"

"Yeah, he's comin' back," said the horse gloomily. "Listen."

The squeals which had got fainter and fainter and died away in the distance had begun again, and were getting louder and louder. "It's like these moving pictures of races," said Georgie, "and then you see them run over again backward." Louder and louder. "Help! Uncle Jinx! Help!" yelled Weedly, and then he was in the barnyard, and he scattered the animals as he dashed through them and disappeared again into the barn.

"There goes *my* night's sleep," grumbled Hank.

"Where on earth is Jinx?" said Mrs. Wiggins. "He's the one to be looking after the poor little creature."

But Jinx had heard the squeals. He had been just dropping off to sleep when they began. "My goodness," he said, jumping up, "it's Little Weedly! I forgot all about him! Oh, I've got to get out of here!"

Jinx didn't waste any time. The only way to get out was through the door, and as he couldn't open it himself, either Aunt Effie or Uncle Snedeker would have to open it for him. He climbed up on a big pile of boxes and began pushing them one after the other on to the floor.

After the bang that each box made in falling, he listened a minute, and at last he heard what he had been waiting for—voices in the hall. He went down close to the door.

"Eh, eh, I'll open it, Effie, I'll open it," he heard Uncle Snedeker say. "But ain't it kind of foolhardy, Effie? Indian warwhoops, that's what those yells were if I ever heard 'em. And then the noises in the attic—that's the way the Indians come; cut a hole in the roof and then creep in, all silent and stealthy, and first thing you know—zip! And you're scalped."

"Nonsense!" said Aunt Effie sharply. "There hasn't been an Indian around here for two hundred years. And if there was, what good would your scalp do 'em, I'd like to know?"

"Eh, that's just it," said Uncle Snedeker.

" 'Tain't myself I'm thinking about. I'm balder'n an old eagle. But your nice long, thick hair—eh, I'd hate to have you lose it, Effie. All the trouble you've had combin' and curlin' it—"

"Snedeker," interrupted Aunt Effie, "open that door!"

There was a pause, and then as the knob turned, Jinx got ready. And when the door slowly opened he dashed through.

Even then he was hardly quick enough. Uncle Snedeker gave a yelp and staggered back, but Aunt Effie was made of sterner stuff. "There's your Indians!" she exclaimed, and swung with her broom. It missed Jinx by the width of his tail, and then he was dashing down the stairs, with Aunt Effie in pursuit.

It was lucky for the cat that the Snedekers had thrown up the front parlor window to see what all the noise was about. He made one bound from the foot of the stairs to the parlor door, another to the windowsill, and the third landed him on the ground and in safety, with Aunt Effie shaking her broomstick at him from the window. At another time Jinx would have sat down in full view of Aunt Effie and calmly washed his face, pretending all the time that he didn't see her, that he never had seen her before, and that he hadn't the slightest interest in anything concerned with her. And he probably would have succeeded in making her good and mad. But now there were other things to attend to. So he went over to the barn.

Little Weedly was cowering in the farthest corner of the box stall. He was about worn out—not so much because he had been running, as because he had been yelling. For yelling is about the hardest exercise there is, and if a lot of people who weigh too much would just yell ten minutes a day, instead of playing golf or tennis or swinging Indian clubs, they would reduce very quickly. Only, of course, the neighbors probably wouldn't like it much.

"Well, well, Weedly," said Jinx, "what's wrong here? Who's been playing tricks on you?"

"Oh, Uncle Jinx," panted Little Weedly, "I'm so glad you're here. It was awful!"

"What was awful?" said Jinx. But Weedly couldn't tell him. It was awful, and it had scared him; that was all he knew.

"Well, you're all right now," said Jinx. "You go to sleep, and I'll be back in a minute. I'm going to get to the bottom of this."

So he went out to get to the bottom of it. The animals were still standing around the barn door. "You fellows ought to be ashamed of yourselves," he said angrily, "playing tricks on a poor little helpless pig."

"Nobody played tricks on him, Jinx," said Robert. "As far as we can make out, he just scared himself, because you'd gone off and left him alone. After all, you adopted him; why didn't you stay with him?"

"Because I had important business to see to, for Mr. Bean," said Jinx.

Henrietta cackled drily. "Yes, we know the kind of important business. Down on the flats chasing frogs, probably. You've got about as much sense of responsibility as—well, as Charles here. I can't put it any stronger than that."

"Oh, come, Henrietta," said Charles, "just

because you asked me to sit on those eggs this afternoon, and I forgot and went down to swim—"

"Now, now," put in Mrs. Wiggins good-naturedly, "one thing at a time. Are we discussing Charles' shortcomings as a husband, or Jinx's shortcomings as a guardian? What was this business, Jinx? You've got something important to tell us, I know."

"Yes, if you'll let me tell it," said Jinx grumpily. "I couldn't be with Weedly because I was locked in the attic." And he told them his story.

The animals were a good deal worried by the news. They had heard from Freddy about the result of the sheriff's visit, and so they knew that the Snedekers really were Mr. Bean's relatives. It was probably going to be unpleasant enough trying to get along with them until the Beans got home, but nobody had supposed that they were really up to any mischief.

"We mustn't let them get that teapot if we can help it," said Mrs. Wiggins. "But I don't see how we can help it. Even if one of us could get in and get it, he certainly couldn't get out with it. Of course, I'm not very good at thinking up things. Maybe one of you animals has got an idea."

"I'm afraid I haven't," said Freddy.

"Land sakes," said Hank, "don't look at *me*!"

"Peter could get in," said Georgie. "He's terrible strong. He could just push the door in and walk upstairs and get the teapot, and then walk out with it. And if she came after him with the broom, he'd just laugh."

"Yes," said Jinx, "and what if, instead of the broom, she picked up Mr. Bean's shotgun? We don't want to spend the rest of the summer picking birdshot out of poor old Peter. No, we can't prevent them getting the teapot. But what we've got to prevent them from doing is taking it back to Ohio. We've got to keep them here either until we can get it away from them and hide it, or until the Beans come home."

"And I know how we can do that," said Freddy suddenly. "Jinx told you what Aunt Effie said; that she thought it was terrible to leave a farm with nobody but the animals to look after it, and that she was going to see that it was properly run. You see, she's one of those people that can't stand it to see things being misused, and not taken care of. Even if they aren't her things. So all we've got to do is make her think everything on the farm is going to pieces, and then she'll stay here until she gets it all in good shape."

"Gosh, that's an idea, Freddy," said Jinx.

"Maybe it is," said Mrs. Wiggins. "Maybe it is. I'm not much good at ideas myself, and that's a fact. You mean, Freddy, that if there's a hole in the barn roof, she'll stay until she gets it mended?"

"Exactly," said Jinx, "and I know just where we can make a hole in the barn roof. It'll keep her busy here for one day, anyway. There's some loose shingles I noticed the other night when I was up there singing."

"Yeah," said Hank, "and I guess maybe it was your singing that loosened them. If I had that gun you were talking about, there'd have been a hole in that song of yours that it would take more than Aunt Effie to patch up."

"Why, Hank," said Jinx with a grin, "don't you like music?"

"Sure," said the horse. "But I thought we were talking about your singing."

Jinx couldn't think of anything to say to that so he just said, "Pooh!" And then after a minute he said: "Well, as I was saying, I can go up and tear some of those shingles out—"

"You're not going to leave that little pig alone any longer," said Mrs. Wiggins firmly. "You brought him here, and you've got to look after him. Though what you're going to do with him, I'm sure I don't know."

"Pooh," said Jinx, "you leave it to me. He'll turn out all right; you wait and see. He's smart, that young one—smart as a whip. He'll get over being so bashful and scared in a little while. We were all that way once ourselves. Why, when I was a kitten—"

"When you were a kitten," said Mrs. Wiggins, "you were the worst nuisance on four legs. You were about as bashful as a pack of firecrackers, and just about as comfortable to have around."

"Oh, that was later," said the cat. "I really

was scared of everything though. And do you know what cured me? I was down playing in the brush-lot with my mother one day. My mother was pretending she was a mouse, and I was jumping out and pretending to scare her. Well, she hid, and I was hunting for her when I saw something come poking through the bushes. I thought it was mother, and I made a jump and landed with all four feet right on your nose. You'd heard something moving in the bushes and had poked your nose in to find out what it was. Ho, ho!" Jinx laughed, "talk about Weedly making a noise! They could hear you over at Witherspoons'."

Mrs. Wiggins smiled, and if you have never seen a cow smile, you don't know how large and comfortable and pleasant a smile can be. "I guess I did make quite a commotion," she said.

"I'll say you did," said Jinx. "And I wasn't ever scared of things after that. When I knew that an animal fifty times as big as I was, was afraid of *me*—" He stopped suddenly. "Golly!" he said. "That's how we can cure

Weedly. If we all pretend to be afraid of
him—"

"Pretend to be afraid of a pig?" exclaimed
Charles, ruffling up his feathers indignantly.

"Sure. When you see him, squawk and run
away and hide. Give him the big build-up."

"Well, I certainly shall do nothing of the
kind," said the rooster. "Why, it's—it's undig-
nified."

"Ha!" said Henrietta. "That's a good one
—from you."

"Let me handle this, Henrietta," said Jinx.
"Come on, Charles, be a sport. Just to please
me. The others will all do it; won't you,
animals?"

" 'Twouldn't be any trouble for me," said
Hank. "I'm scared of the critter now." And
Freddy and Robert and the other animals
said, well yes, they'd try it.

But Mrs. Wiggins shook her head. "I don't
know, Jinx," she said. "I'm willing to do anything within reason. But I can't go cavorting
off over the hills in hysterics every time I see
him. How would it be if I just look startled?"

"How do you look when you look startled?" the cat asked, and Mrs. Wiggins thought a minute, and then she opened her eyes wide and dropped her jaw and waggled her ears. "Guess that's about it," she said.

"Good gracious!" said Jinx. "You'd scare him to death!"

"H'm," said Mrs. Wiggins. "Well, how's this?" And she suddenly sat down weakly, and closed her eyes, and put one front hoof to her heart and said: "Oh! Oh, dear! Oh, dear me!"

"Splendid!" said Freddy. "Mrs. Wiggins, you're a born actor. My goodness, that gives me an idea. Good night, you fellows." And he trotted off toward the pigpen.

"That's what it is to be a poet," said the cat disgustedly. "Right in the middle of something, you get an idea and have to go write it down, and leave the other fellow to do the work. Well, anyway, I guess it's all settled that you'll help me out with Weedly. I know it'll be a nuisance, but he's a swell little pig, really. And I know you'll help him a lot. Besides, you'll be doing something for me.

And I don't ask favors of you very often."

"No, that's true, Jinx," said Henrietta. "You can count on the chickens—and that includes Charles, of course." And she moved over beside her husband and smoothed down a feather on the side of his head with her beak.

Charles started, and eyed her suspiciously. Her beak was very close to his ear, and although a rooster's ear isn't large, it is very sensitive. "Well," he said, "I—er, that is, certainly, Jinx. I am only too pleased to take any steps which would tend to ameliorate the conditions surrounding the education of your adopted nephew, and I will say here and now—"

"Don't make a speech," said Henrietta sharply.

"—that I—er, that is, you can count on me," concluded Charles.

"Fine," said Jinx. "And now that's settled, I'll go fix that roof. Don't worry—I'll take Weedly along so he won't cause any more trouble."

Chapter 4

Jinx took Little Weedly up the narrow barn stairs into the loft, and then he climbed out on the roof and began to loosen the shingles. Every now and then he would call down: "Are you all right, Weedly?" and the pig would answer: "All right, Uncle Jinx." As soon as the hole was big enough, Jinx dropped down through it.

"I guess that'll give Aunt Effie something to do tomorrow," he said. "Now we'll go down to the box stall and get some sleep."

An hour or so later, a dark cloud came rolling silently across the sky. One by one the stars went out; the night got darker, and a cool damp feeling came into the air. Up in the woods all the little animals stirred, and snuggled closer into their nests, and Peter, the bear, woke up and sniffed. "H'm," he grunted. "Rain." So he got up and lumbered off to the shallow cave in the rocks where he took shelter in stormy weather. For he knew the birds would not steal his berries if it rained.

But the farm animals, who slept under roofs, did not wake up, even after the stars had all gone out, and the first raindrops pattered like mice running over the shingles. In the barn, Hank slept standing up, and next door in the box stall, Jinx and Weedly snoozed away side by side. The patter grew to a soft and steady rushing sound, and pretty soon there were little gurglings and splashings as the water ran into the eaves trough and down into the rain barrel at the corner of the barn. And under all these sounds was a steady drip-drip-drip, that got faster and faster. And that was the rain coming down through the hole in the shingles.

It dripped down on to the floor of the loft, and it ran along a crack between two boards until it came to a knothole, and it went down through the knothole and dripped on the middle of Hank's back. And then it ran down Hank's left hind leg, and where it went after that I don't know.

Pretty soon Hank woke up with a snort. He had been dreaming that he was out skating—something of course that he had never done in his life—and that the ice had given way. He struggled and struggled to get to the surface, and suddenly his head popped out, and he was awake and listening to the rain dripping on his back.

"Consarn it!" he said. "It would have to be *my* roof they made a hole in! Darn that Jinx! If he's awake, I'll make him go up and stuff some hay in that hole."

He whispered Jinx's name several times, but the cat didn't answer.

"And if I call him louder," said Hank to himself, "that crazy pig will wake up and commence squealing. And my nerves just won't stand that again." He stood thinking for a

minute, and the rain dripped faster. "Ideas!"
he said disgustedly. "There's too many ideas
around here if you ask me." And then he said:
"Well, I suppose I can move. That's an idea
too, I suppose."

He backed out of his stall, trying to walk
on tiptoes, which is a pretty hard thing for a
horse to do. But he managed not to make
much noise. He went over and stood behind
the old phaeton, which he had drawn all the
way back from Florida the year the animals
had taken their famous trip south. Since he
usually slept standing up, you wouldn't think
it mattered very much where he did it. But
lots of people find it hard to sleep in a strange
bed, and probably it was that way with Hank.
He was restless, and finally, when the rain
began to slacken, he thought: "If I stand
around wet like this, it isn't going to help the
rheumatism in my off hind leg. I'll be as stiff
as a saw-horse in the morning." So he went
out for a walk.

When he came back, the sky in the east was
all pink, and as he passed the henhouse he
heard Henrietta's voice. "This is the third

time I've called you. Now you take your head out from under your wing and get on out there."

There was a sleepy mumble from Charles, and Henrietta said: "If Mr. Bean's away, all the more reason why you should do your duty. Come along. Out you go." There was a fluttering and squawking, and then the door flew open and Charles came tumbling out.

The rooster's feathers were tousled, and he looked nervously over his shoulder as he walked toward the fence. But as he shook his feathers down he caught sight of Hank, and at once he threw out his chest and began to strut pompously. "Good morning, Hank; good morning," he said. "Excuse me one moment." And he climbed up on the fence and crowed. Then he said: "Have to do this regular as clockwork every morning, you know, or things wouldn't get started right. It's a great responsibility, in a way, but so far I think I can say I have always done my duty." He crowed again. "Mr. Bean expects every animal to do his duty," he said solemnly.

"I guess Henrietta does, too," Hank remarked.

"Oh, you heard that, did you?" said Charles. "Yes, Henrietta is very conscientious. She's always afraid I'm not going to get out here in time. You know how women are! But, my goodness, I was all ready. I'd have been out here all right." He crowed again. "You'll excuse me, Hank, but I'll have to go on singing for a while. Dear me, I'm in very good voice this morning." And he crowed some more.

"You and Jinx!" Hank grumbled. "There's too much singing around here, if you ask me. And now that young Weedly has tuned up, too. You ought to get up a quartet and charge admission."

"I'm afraid you don't know much about music, Hank," said the rooster. "You have to have four for a quartet."

"Well, good grief, it ought to be easy to get a fourth. All you have to do is be able to yell. I can yell myself, if it comes to that."

"But it isn't just yelling," said Charles, and

he crowed again. "You see? It's a song. You have to sing the first notes just so, and then the last has to be a long, clear, beautiful note that dies away into silence. Gay, but with just a little touch of sadness, if you know what I mean. Listen." And he crowed again.

"Yeah," said Hank. "It's beautiful, all right. But now you listen to *me*." He threw up his head and opened his mouth and let out a long, shrill neigh.

"Good gracious, Hank," exclaimed the rooster, "don't. *Don't!*"

"Gay enough for you?" asked Hank. "And I hope you noticed the sadness. That comes in at the end. Listen; I'll show you." And he neighed again.

But Charles had had enough. He tumbled off the fence and legged it for the henhouse, from which a number of startled heads were peering. Hank neighed once more for good measure, and then he trotted toward the barn. "Music, eh?" he said. "I'll give 'em music."

But Hank's musical efforts had startled others besides Charles and his family. In the house, Aunt Effie and Uncle Snedeker had been sound asleep. Charles' crowing had awakened them, and they were just thinking about getting up when Hank neighed the first time.

"What's that?" said Aunt Effie, and she jumped up and ran to the window.

"What's that?" said Uncle Snedeker, and he pulled the bedclothes up over his head.

Then Hank neighed twice more.

Aunt Effie continued to stare out of the window, and after a minute she said: "Snedeker, there's a horse down by the henhouse. He must have got out in the night. Go on down and get him into the barn." But of course Uncle Snedeker didn't hear her, because his ears were under a sheet and two patchwork quilts and a down comfortable.

"Snedeker!" said Aunt Effie again, and then she turned around and saw that Uncle Snedeker was only a mound under the bedclothes. So she came and pulled the bedclothes off.

"Indians!" moaned Uncle Snedeker. "That was the warwhoop. They're coming, Effie. Eh, we'll all be murdered in our beds."

"You will, if you don't get out and catch that horse," said Aunt Effie, and she yanked him out and pulled him over to the window. "See him?" He must have got out in the night." And she pointed to Hank, who was trotting toward the barn.

"Eh, Effie," mumbled Uncle Snedeker, "but that's the way they come. They hang down on the other side of the horse, and shoot at you under his neck. You want to send me out to be murdered?"

Aunt Effie let go of him and shook her head. "Seems to me," she said, "you're old enough to stop playing Indians. Well, go on back to bed. I'll get him myself." And she put on a blue flannel bathrobe with yellow stripes, and a pair of slippers with pink bows, and she tied a red shawl over her curlpapers and picked up her broom and went out.

But by the time she had done all that, Hank was back in the barn.

Now most animals are accustomed to being waited on by humans, and so they get out of the habit of doing things for themselves. But the animals on the Bean farm had wanted to help Mr. Bean all they could, and so, even when the Beans were home, they looked after themselves, and even did most of the farm work. So Hank was used to doing his own housekeeping. He went over to the oat bin and lifted the cover with his nose, and started to eat his breakfast. Just then Aunt Effie came into the barn.

Aunt Effie didn't know much about horses, but she did know that they shouldn't be allowed to help themselves to oats.

"Here, here!" she said. "Get back in your stall, you!" And she brandished her broom threateningly.

Hank hadn't finished, but he knew he could go back to the bin after she had gone, so he went into his stall. Aunt Effie scooped up a measure of oats, and poured it into his manger. "Poor creature!" she said. "No wonder you got in the oat bin. What a way to treat animals!" Then she saw the water that had leaked down through the floor above. She went upstairs, and Hank heard her walking around in the loft. Pretty soon she came down and went in the house, and after a while Uncle

Snedeker came out. He had his big, wide-brimmed hat on, and was carrying a ladder and a hammer and nails. He found some shingles in the barn, and then he climbed up and started to patch the roof. He didn't work very fast, because his hat brim was so wide that nearly every time he raised the hammer he knocked it off. Usually it rolled off the roof to the ground, and then he had to climb down and put it on again. After a while, though, he discovered that if he tilted the hat over to the left, the hammer didn't hit the brim on the way up. But every now and then, on the way down, it hit his thumb. He wasn't a very good carpenter.

Jinx and Little Weedly, who had been sleeping late, were disturbed by the hammering, and by Uncle Snedeker's remarks when he hit his thumb, so they got up, and were just going down to see Freddy, when Freddy came in the door.

"Morning, boys," said the pig. "Say, Hank, you were going to mow the upper meadow today, weren't you?"

"Well," said Hank, "I sort of calculated to.

If somebody'll help hitch me up to the mowing machine.''

"Well, now look," said Freddy. "We don't want Aunt Effie to think we can run this farm. Let the hay go. Then I'll write a note on my typewriter, and leave it in the mail box. Something like this:

"Dear Madam:

The hay in the upper meadow must be mowed right away. Maybe it's none of my business if Mr. Bean wants to let his farm go to rack and ruin, but I can't stand by and see good hay spoiled.

From an Admirer.

"Then, you see, she'll feel that she ought to stay until the hay is all cut and in the barn, and that'll take several days. After that we can think of something else."

"That's a good idea, Freddy," said Jinx. "But why did you sign it 'Admirer'? Why not just 'Friend'?"

"Oh, I don't know," said the pig. "I thought it would make her more anxious to get the hay in, for one thing. If you think somebody appreciates what you do, you like doing it better. And then, you know, I do sort of admire her, at that. She may be trying to steal that teapot, but on the other hand, she didn't have to patch the barn roof."

"She was real upset when she thought I hadn't had enough to eat," said Hank.

"I guess she's good in spots, like a lot of people," said Jinx. "I had a cousin like that. He lived with old Miss Halsey, down in Centerboro. If ever a cat was a saint, he was. He chased the mice out of the house, and he always sat in her lap and purred, even when he wanted to go hunting. And yet, every time she went out, he went up into the spare bedroom and curled up on her best lace counterpane."

"Don't see what difference it made, as long as she didn't find out," said Hank.

"It wasn't very good for the counterpane," said Jinx. "And she did find out, too. One day he jumped down quick when he heard her coming in the front door, and he caught a claw in the lace and couldn't get loose. He struggled and struggled, but the harder he tried, the more he got wound up in the lace. Miss Halsey heard him, and she came upstairs and found him."

"What did she do?" Freddy asked.

"I don't know. He never would talk about that afterward."

"Well," said Freddy, "as long as you think it's a good idea, I'll go write that letter and get it in the mail box before the mail man comes along. And if either of you think of anything else, to keep the Snedekers busy, let me know." And he trotted off toward the pigpen.

"Come along, Weedly," said the cat. "We'll go over to the cowbarn and see if Mrs. Wiggins has heard anything from Mr. Webb yet. Though I don't suppose she has. Webb won't start out before the dew's off the grass."

Little Weedly, who had been trying to hide behind Jinx during the talk with Freddy and Hank, gave a sigh. "Now—do we have to go see the cows, Uncle Jinx? I—I don't like cows very well."

"Pooh," said Jinx. "Everybody likes Mrs. Wiggins. She's got a heart of gold. And so have Mrs. Wurzburger and Mrs. Wogus. Come along."

Weedly didn't say any more, but when he came to the door of the cowbarn he drooped his ears, and the curl came out of his tail, and he pressed tight against Jinx.

The three cows were standing with their backs to the door, but at Jinx's loud "good morning" they turned around, and when they saw Little Weedly, all three sat down suddenly, and closed their eyes, and put their right front hoofs over their hearts, and said: "Oh! Oh, dear! Oh, dear me!"

Jinx had a hard time not to giggle, but he managed to keep a straight face. "Well, well," he said, "what's the matter?"

"Oh!" gasped Mrs. Wurzburger, opening one eye, "take that ferocious animal out of here before I faint!"

"Why, good gracious," said Jinx, "it's only Freddy's cousin, Little Weedly, who has come over to pay us a visit."

"Take him away!" said Mrs. Wiggins without opening her eyes. "Oh, the great glaring eyes of him!"

"Oh! Oh, dear! Oh, dear me."

"What's the matter with them, Uncle Jinx?" asked Weedly, looking over the cat's shoulder.

"Oh, that great voice!" groaned Mrs. Wogus. "It's like the roaring of lions!" And then Mrs. Wiggins rolled right over on her side, apparently in a dead faint.

"I guess we'd better get out of here," said Jinx. Indeed he wanted to laugh so badly that he knew if he didn't get out he would spoil the effect of the whole show. He led Weedly outside. "I guess they were afraid of you, Weedly," he said.

"But what are they afraid of me for?" asked the pig. He didn't seem to want to leave the cowbarn, and he kept turning around and looking over his shoulder.

"I'm sure I don't know," said the cat. "I expect they thought you might bite them. You do look pretty determined, you know."

"Do I really?" said Weedly. "But I wouldn't bite them. I—I sort of liked them, Uncle Jinx. Couldn't we go back now? Maybe they'd feel better if you told them that I wouldn't hurt them."

"Later, perhaps," said Jinx. Weedly had stopped pressing close to him, and was trotting along beside him almost self-confidently. "You see," said Jinx, "most of the animals on this farm are a little timid with strangers. I thought we might look in on one or two of the others, so they'll get to know you. They'll probably be a little scared of you at first, so I'd be very quiet and not say very much until they know you better. Let's go down to the pond and have a chat with the ducks. Maybe they'll invite you to have a swim."

"Will they be scared of me?" asked Weedly.

"They're pretty bashful," said Jinx, "but you just act as if you didn't notice it, and it'll pass off. It always does."

"Does it? I've always been pretty bashful myself, Uncle Jinx."

"Have you really?" said the cat. "I should never have suspected it. No," he said thoughtfully, "to me you seemed quite sure of yourself. I should have imagined that you'd be at home in any company—sort of all things to all animals. That's why I invited you to come over and stay with me. Of course, you acted bashful when Freddy and I came over to your house, but I thought you were just doing that to please your mother.

"And of course you must remember," he said, "that everybody is a little bashful. I suppose you wouldn't believe it, but I am, myself."

Jinx's whiskers twitched when he said this, and well they might, for if ever there was a cat who hadn't an ounce of bashfulness in him from the tip of his black nose to the tip of his black tail, that cat was Jinx. But fortunately Little Weedly didn't know that a cat's whiskers always twitch when he isn't telling the truth. For that matter, perhaps you didn't know it either. But next time you suspect that your cat is not telling you the truth, you watch his whiskers.

Chapter 5

While Jinx was taking Little Weedly around
to call on some of the other animals, Aunt
Effie finished up her housework. Then she
looked out of the window to make sure that
Uncle Snedeker was doing what she had told
him to, and then she went up in the attic to
hunt for the teapot. She opened chests and
barrels and boxes and trunks. She found a
lot of queer things, as anyone does who hunts
around in an attic, and at last she came to the
old horsehide trunk.

On a shelf over the trunk was a toy steam engine that Mr. Bean used to play with when he was a little boy. Mr. and Mrs. Webb were sitting in the engineer's seat, looking out. They often sat there, because they were very fond of travel, and they could imagine that they were steaming off across the countryside at sixty miles an hour to visit strange distant lands. Mr. Webb was the engineer and Mrs. Webb was the passenger. "All aboard," Mr. Webb would say: "All aboard for Persia, Mesopotamia, China and points east." Then, after a minute he would say: "Here we are, mother. Just pulling into the station at Samarkand. See those Arabs there on the camels—that's a caravan of rubies and pearls from the Persian Gulf." And Mrs. Webb would say: "My land, father, let's stop them and buy a couple of quarts to take home to Mrs. Bean." They had lots of fun that way, and Mrs. Webb always said it was much the best way to travel. There was no bother of tickets, or catching trains, and you always slept in your own bed at night. And when you got tired of traveling, you just stopped, and there you were at home.

When Aunt Effie came up into the attic, the Webbs were touring in the Desert of Sahara, but they stopped the tour right away and watched her. When she came to the horsehide trunk, she started to open it, and then she paused. "Goodness!" she said. "Look at those cobwebs all over the lock! That trunk can't have been opened in years. Well, the teapot can't be in there."

Mr. and Mrs. Webb giggled delightedly. They had spent half the night spinning those webs just to make the trunk look as if it hadn't been opened in a long time. It was a smart idea, all right, but they hadn't counted on the fact that Aunt Effie was such a good housekeeper. She took her broom and swept the cobwebs off the trunk. And then she said: "Well, I might as well see what's in it, anyway."

Three minutes later she had rushed out to the barn with the teapot in her hand, and was holding it up triumphantly for Uncle Snedeker to see.

And three minutes after that, every animal

on the farm knew that the teapot was in the hands of the enemy.

Aunt Effie didn't hide the teapot away. She got out Mrs. Bean's best tea cups and arranged them on a little table in the parlor as if for a teaparty, and she put down the teapot in the middle of them. She looked at them for a while, smiling and rubbing her hands, and then she sat down and practiced pouring out imaginary tea for imaginary guests.

She was interrupted in this pleasant occupation by the sound of a car stopping at the gate. It was the mailman, so she went out to speak to him.

"Good morning," said the mail man. "Why! Are the Beans home?"

"No," said Aunt Effie. "I'm Mr. Bean's aunt. We're staying here while they're away."

"I suppose you wonder why I'm stopping here, then," said the man. "But there's always a picture postcard from some foreign place for one of the animals. Mrs. Bean certainly is fond of those animals! There's one for Freddy this morning."

"For the *animals*!" exclaimed Aunt Effie.

"You mean she—she *writes* to them?"

"See for yourself," said the man, handing her the postcard.

It was a picture of the Eiffel Tower in Paris, and on it Mrs. Bean had written: "This is quite a nice place, only Mr. Bean can't get his Pride of the Farm pipe mixture here, and you know he never smokes anything else. Lovely weather. Wish you were with us."

" 'Wish you were with us'!" said Aunt Effie. "A pig in Paris! Well, that would be just fine!"

The mail man looked at her curiously, and then he said: "Well, I must be getting on."

"Just a minute," said Aunt Effie. "I wonder if you can tell me who our nearest neighbors are? I—well, I thought it would be nice to give some of the ladies a little teaparty—to get acquainted with them, you know. We didn't get here until after the Beans had left, so I couldn't ask them. But I suppose you'd know."

The mail man shook his head. "Most of the folks around here are too busy to go in for teaparties much. There's Mrs. Witherspoon, over the hill. But she hasn't been out of the house in ten years. Don't get time. There's old Miss McQuee. But she don't ever drink anything but coffee. No ma'am, this isn't very good teaparty territory, and that's the truth."

He drove off. As Aunt Effie turned to go into the house she caught sight of the note Freddy had left in the mail box. She took it out and read it. Then she hurried across to the barn.

"Snedeker!" she called to her husband. "Haven't you finished that roof yet?"

Uncle Snedeker stopped with the hammer raised and looked down. "Eh, just a minute, Effie. Just till I pound this nail." He brought the hammer down and said: "Ouch!" and stuck his thumb in his mouth. Then he took it out and looked at it. "Pounded the wrong nail that time," he said. "Eh, Effie—you get that? Hit the thumbnail instead of the shingle nail. Get it?"

"Come down here," she commanded.

" 'Taint everybody that could make a joke when he'd just hit his thumb," grumbled

Uncle Snedeker. "Good joke, too. Eh, well, what is it?"

She handed him the note. " 'Admirer,' eh?" he said when he had read it.

"Yes," said Aunt Effie, trying not to look pleased. "An admirer," she repeated, looking over his shoulder. "Now I wonder who that could be?"

"I can't imagine," said Uncle Snedeker.

She straightened up. "Oh, you can't," she said sarcastically. "You find it strange that anybody should admire me, do you? I guess there are plenty of people back in Orenville that admire me. I guess nobody gives any better teaparties than I do, do they?"

"No, no, Effie," protested Uncle Snedeker. "Eh, gosh, all I meant was that there ain't anybody around here that *knows* you. Soon as they know you they admire you. But we haven't met anybody but the sheriff. Maybe it's the sheriff."

"I suppose it must be," said Aunt Effie thoughtfully. "Such a nice man, too, except for that foolishness about talking animals. I must ask him to tea. Dear me 'an admirer'! How courtly of him!" She twittered and blushed, and then she stiffened her back and said: "Anyway, Snedeker, you'll have to mow that meadow."

"Me?" exclaimed Uncle Snedeker. "I don't know any more about mowing machines than I do about fancy work. You've got the teapot now, Effie. Why don't we go back home?"

"Not while there are things that need attention. I'm not going to have William Bean saying that I neglected his place while I was here. You'll have to cut that hay."

"Cut my leg off, like as not," grumbled Uncle Snedeker.

"Cut 'em both off if you want to. But you'll mow it, legs or no legs. And when you go down that way," she added, "deliver this postcard at the pigpen."

"At the *what*?" demanded Uncle Snedeker, looking at the card. "Why, shine my Sunday shoes! She's written a postcard to a pig!"

"Yes," said Aunt Effie. "It beats all how silly some people can act. I felt sort of bad, taking that teapot away from her, even though it should have come to me, but not now, I don't. Why, she isn't worthy of having a fine silver teapot like that."

"But what do you want it delivered for, eh? 'Tisn't any use to a pig."

"Maybe not," said Aunt Effie. "But even though it's kind of silly, you take it down. It isn't for us to inquire whether the pig can read it or not."

So on his way over to the shed where the mowing machine was kept, Uncle Snedeker stopped at the pigpen. He started to knock on the door, and then hesitated. "Darned if I'll knock on any pig's door," he said, and stuffed the card in the crack and went on.

In the meantime, Jinx and Little Weedly had had a very successful morning. They had called on the ducks and the dogs; on Charles and Henrietta, and on John, the fox, who had a summer home in the orchard. Everywhere the animals had played up, and pretended to be terrified at the sight of Weedly; and as a result the pig had already lost a lot of his timidity. He no longer pressed tight against

Jinx as they walked along. His manner at times was almost cocky. Jinx was very much pleased.

As they came back from the orchard, they had to cross a corner of the upper meadow. Uncle Snedeker had managed to hitch Hank to the mowing machine, and was just making his first cut along the stone wall. He was coming right towards them.

Little Weedly was getting over his fear of other animals, but a man on a mowing machine was something different. He gave a squeal and ducked down into the long grass.

"Come out of there, Weedly," called Jinx. "You're right in the path of the machine. Get up on the wall till he gets by."

But Weedly wasn't going to come out where he could be seen. He began to crawl through the grass away from the machine.

Uncle Snedeker was jouncing along on the iron seat, holding the reins in one hand, and hanging onto his hat, which kept sliding down over his nose, with the other. The mowing machine kept up a pleasant clatter, but noises are only pleasant when you are used to them,

. . . he bent forward and looked at the ripple . . .

and it didn't seem pleasant to Uncle Snedeker. He wasn't used to cutting hay, and to him it sounded like the snip-snip of dozens of hungry little pairs of scissors, only waiting until he finally lost his balance and fell off, to chop him into mincemeat. He wasn't used to farms or farming, either, and his eyes kept roaming back and forth across the fields and the edge of the woods, for he didn't know what strange animals might suddenly leap out at him. Wolves, perhaps, or even Indians.

And then he caught sight of the ripple in the grass that Little Weedly made as he crawled along on his stomach.

"Whoa!" said Uncle Snedeker, and when Hank stopped, he bent forward and looked at the ripple under the flat of his hand, as he had seen cowboys do in the movies. "Eh, that's the way they come," he muttered, "with a tomahawk in one hand, and a bow in the other. And then when they get close enough, up they jump with a whoop—"

Just at that minute Weedly stepped on a hoptoad. The toad made a sound which would probably be spelled as something like "unkh!" Weedly made a sound, too, as he jumped up, but it isn't one that anybody could possibly spell. It was one of his biggest and best squeals. And Uncle Snedeker gave a yell, and jumped down from the mowing machine, and ran for his life toward the house.

Chapter 6

Uncle Snedeker was usually considered to be a pretty good husband. That is, he almost always did what Aunt Effie told him to. But once in a while he got stubborn, and then she couldn't do anything with him. This was one of the times. He refused absolutely to go out again into the meadow. So after arguing with him for a while, Aunt Effie went out to mow the hay herself.

Aunt Effie had her own ideas of what was

right and proper. On her tenth birthday, her mother had given her an etiquette book, and all her life she had done what the etiquette book said was the correct thing to do. So it can't be denied that she had good manners. But of course her tenth birthday was a long time ago, and the manners she got from the etiquette book were rather old-fashioned. She would no more have thought of going out of the house without a hat and coat on than you would think of eating soup with a fork. So when she went up and climbed into the seat of the mowing machine, she had on her second-best bonnet and shawl.

Hank's manners weren't very polished, but he was polite, and although he turned around and looked at her several times, he didn't laugh. And he walked along very slowly and carefully, so that she shouldn't fall off.

So that morning Aunt Effie mowed the whole of the upper meadow, and after she had had her dinner, she hitched Hank to the rake and raked all the hay into heaps and left it there to dry in the hot sun. And then she had supper, and changed to her best bonnet and shawl, and told Uncle Snedeker that he could drive her down to Centerboro to the movies. "I've worked hard all day," she said, "and I need a little relaxation."

Freddy had been working hard all that day, too. When Mrs. Wiggins had put her hoof over her heart and pretended to be frightened, it had given him an idea. He thought he would write a play. He thought it would be a good play with Mrs. Wiggins as the heroine, and it would be exciting, and most of the other animals would have parts. And when he had it written, they could give it in the barn. Only he didn't know what the play would be about.

It is pretty hard to write a play if you don't know what it is about, and so all Freddy had written down on the sheet of paper in his typewriter was:

A PLAY

by

FREDDY

Act I.

He was still sitting in front of the type-writer at three o'clock, when Jinx and Little Weedly stopped in. Most people are not as much afraid of their relatives as of strangers, and Weedly walked right in without trembling, and he hardly blushed at all when he said: "Good afternoon, Cousin Frederick."

"I hope we're not disturbing you," said Jinx with a grin. "If we are, just say so, and we'll keep right on doing it."

"Well, as a matter of fact," said Freddy, "I've been working hard all day, and I'm glad to rest a little."

"I should think you would be," said Jinx, looking over his shoulder. "Do you mean to tell me that you've done all that today?"

"There's more to writing a play than just putting it down on paper," protested Freddy. "I want to write one that you can all have parts in—you and Mrs. Wiggins and Hank and Charles and Robert and all the rest of us."

"That would be fun," said the cat. "But why write one? Why don't we put on one that's already written? You've got a whole book of plays here by that what's-his-name—

the fellow you always claim wrote the best plays that ever were written?"

"Oh, you mean Shakespeare," said Freddy, who was a great reader of the works of that author. "Well, we could, but I thought it would be more fun to write and put on our own play, all by ourselves. Then, you see, everybody could act out a character that he liked. Now me, for instance; I've done a lot of detective work, and I could be Sherlock Holmes. And you could be—"

"A G-man," interrupted Jinx. "Sure, that's a great idea. And look here, Freddy, why don't you let everybody choose a character they'd like to be, and then you write a play about them?"

"Gosh, Jinx, I think you've got something there! Yes, sir, you certainly have. It'll be kind of mixed up, because some of the characters will be modern, and some will be a couple of hundred years old. You know who Mrs. Wiggins will want to be—Queen Elizabeth. But I guess we can work it. Let's see— how about you, Weedly? Who do you want to be?"

But Little Weedly had curled up in a corner and gone to sleep.

"Golly, I hope he isn't going to be like his father," said Jinx. "Just a yawn on four legs, that Ernest. But I guess it's because he didn't get much sleep last night. Anyway, I don't believe we'd ever get him to act."

"If he keeps on improving at the rate he has today, we could," said Freddy.

"Yes, but he's only met animals that pretended to be afraid of him today. I don't know what will happen when he meets strangers. I thought maybe while he's still feeling so sure of himself, I'd take him down to the movies in Centerboro tonight. What do you think?"

Most animals don't have much use for pocket money, simply because they don't have any pockets. When they find pennies and dimes and nickels—and they find more than you would believe—they haven't any place to save them up. But when Freddy had founded the First Animal Bank of Centerboro, all this changed. By the time the bank had been running a year, nearly all the Bean animals had nice little bank accounts.

Of course they didn't have as much use for money as boys and girls have, because Mr. Bean got them everything they needed. But they did like to go to the movies, and so now they could go when they wanted to. Mr. Muszkiski, who ran the Grand Palace Motion Picture Theatre in Centerboro, liked to have them come, too, because a pig and a horse and a couple of squirrels in the audience is an added attraction to any film, and a great many people came just to see the animals. So animals were only charged half price, which was ten cents.

Freddy wasn't sure whether it would be wise to take Little Weedly to the movies or not. "If the people crowd around and stare and laugh, as they do sometimes," he said, "it may scare him again, and then he'll be bashful all the rest of his life.—But wait a minute! I know what we can do."

He rummaged around in the heaps of old newspapers and magazines on his desk, and found a stick of black grease paint that he had used in disguising himself when he had been doing detective work. Then he very cautiously knelt down in front of Little Weedly and painted a big black moustache and heavy black eyebrows on the sleeper's face.

"That ought to scare 'em," he said.

"Golly, doesn't he look fierce!" said Jinx, and began to giggle.

"Wait till the sheriff sees him," said Freddy. "He'll arrest him on sight." And he began to giggle too.

They giggled so hard finally that Weedly woke up and asked them what they were laughing at.

"Oh, nothing," said Jinx, "nothing. Just something your Cousin Frederick thought of. By the way, Freddy, I'll have to draw some money out of the First Animal for movie tickets."

"The bank's open this afternoon," said Freddy. "I'm going down there now."

So they walked down to the bank, which was in an old shed at the side of the road. There was no door on the bank but none was needed, for all the money and valuables were kept in the underground vaults which the woodchucks and John, the fox, had dug. The opening to the vaults was covered with an old plank, which was guarded night and day by two squirrels.

As Freddy came in, the squirrels got up from the plank, on which they had been sitting, and said respectfully: "Good morning, Mr. President."

"Good morning, boys, good morning," said Freddy affably. He went back of the long counter, put on a pair of spectacles which made him look very responsible and bank-presidentish, and opened a large book.

"Let me see," he said, "let me see. Jinx, Jinx, Jinx—ah, here it is. According to our books, Jinx, you have a balance of exactly forty-six cents, two bunches of dried catnip, and a rubber mouse. In that case I think we can let you have twenty cents—yes, I think we can. Boys—" he turned to the squirrels—"go down and get twenty cents for Mr. Jinx. And at the same time, bring up a dime for me."

The squirrels tugged the plank aside and dove down the hole.

"Why did you say good morning, Freddy?"

asked Jinx. "It's nearly four o'clock."

"Well, you see," said the pig, "the bank's really supposed to be open mornings, but I'm so busy that I seldom get down until afternoon. It doesn't make any difference really. But if someone was to complain about it, I'd just turn to the squirrels and say: 'What do I always say to you boys when I come in?' And they'd say: 'Why, you always say good morning.' And then whoever complained wouldn't have any comeback to that."

"But they *know* you're not here mornings, Cousin Frederick," said Weedly.

"What you know, and what you can prove, are two very different things," Freddy said.

"Yes," said Little Weedly, "but—"

"Don't argue with him, Weedly," said Jinx. "Why, talk about proving things: he can prove that the moon is made of green cheese. He could even prove that you had a long black moustache, if he wanted to."

"I guess you couldn't prove that very well, Cousin Frederick," said Weedly, laughing.

"Well, I'm not going to try, not right now anyway," Freddy answered. "And here are the boys with the money. Run along now; I must enter these transactions in the book. See you at the show."

When they had gone, Freddy wrote for a while. Then he said to the squirrels: "You boys can take a little nap if you want to. I'll be here, and I'll see that no burglars get in." So the squirrels curled up and went to sleep, and Freddy, after watching them closely for a few minutes, put his head down on the counter and went to sleep too.

If any burglars had come, they could have cleaned out that bank—lock, stock and barrel —capital, resources and personnel. Only of course they would have had to be small enough burglars to get down into the vaults, and the only burglars Freddy had ever seen were much too large, so he felt perfectly safe.

By and by he woke up, and he thought for a while about plans for keeping Aunt Effie on the farm until they could get back the teapot, and then he thought about his play. And then he woke up the watchmen and went back home to supper. When he got there, he found that he still had on his spectacles.

The spectacles just had windowglass in them and were only for show. He never wore them anywhere but in the bank. "If I keep them around here, they'll get lost," he thought. "I'll wear them to the movies, and stop in and leave them at the bank when I come home." So after supper he started out.

It was a midsummer evening, and the sun was close to setting as he trudged down the dusty road to Centerboro. Under the roadside maples it was beginning to get dark, and indeed, after the first mile, it seemed to be getting dark much more quickly than usual. One or two cars passed him, nearly choking him with dust, and then a big gravel truck thundered past. When the dust from that had drifted away, the sky seemed suddenly to have become overcast. "Going to have a storm," he thought, and trotted along faster. More cars passed him, bound for Centerboro and the movies; it was getting so dark that he could hardly see the road. And then from ahead a voice hailed him.

"Hello, Freddy."

Freddy peered around, but could make out

nothing in the gloom. "Who is it?" he said. "It's so dark I can't see you."

"Dark!" said the voice. "What are you talking about? It's me—Jinx."

"Oh," said Freddy. "Well, I guess we shouldn't have started for the movies. There's going to be a terrible storm. Did you ever know it to get dark so quick? Let's not waste any time; maybe we can get there before it begins to rain."

Jinx began to laugh, and Freddy heard Little Weedly snicker. "I don't see what's so funny—" he began.

"That's just it," said Jinx. "You can't see anything. Well, you know I can see in the dark pretty well. Just catch hold of my tail and I'll lead you."

"I guess I'll have to," said Freddy. "I can't see a thing now. But I don't see what you're laughing at."

"Just a little joke we had," said Jinx. "Catch hold."

So Freddy took hold of Jinx's tail and stumbled along behind him for another mile. Then the cat stopped. "Guess you'll have to walk the rest of the way without help," he said.

"What's the matter?" Freddy asked. "We were getting along all right. Of course if you want to go on ahead—if you're afraid of getting wet, why go on. But I can't possibly keep on the road in this darkness."

"Oh, yes you can," said the cat. "I know it, and I can prove it, too." And he snatched Freddy's spectacles off.

"My goodness!" the pig exclaimed. "Why, it isn't dark at all. It's—I—" He stopped and looked at the spectacles. "Well, I'll be darned!" he said, as he saw what had happened. For the dust whipped up from the road by the passing cars had settled thicker and thicker on the lenses, until they were so coated that no light could get through. Then he looked at Jinx. "And you made me walk that whole mile, holding on to your tail"

"I could have made you walk the whole way, if I'd wanted to," said Jinx. "But a joke's a joke. Come on, polish your spectacles and let's get going."

"What'll I polish them with?" asked Freddy.

"If you wear glasses, you certainly have to carry a pocket handkerchief to polish them with."

"A pocket handkerchief!" said Freddy disgustedly. "I haven't got a pocket handkerchief, and if I did, I haven't got anything to carry it in." He looked at the spectacles and shook his head. "Oh, no," he said, "nothing doing. If I have a handkerchief, I have to have a pocket to carry it in, and if I have a pocket, I have to have a suit to sew it in, and if I have a suit, I have to have a closet to hang it in, and if I have a closet, I have to have a house—Rats!" he said, and tossed the spectacles into the bushes. "Come on. I never did like the things anyway."

At the edge of town they began to meet people. Nearly everybody in Centerboro knew Mr. Bean's animals, and there were nods and smiles as they passed by, and one little boy even took his hat off to Freddy. Little Weedly was walking between, and just a little behind the other two animals, so no-

. . . picked her up and whacked her on the back.

body noticed him, but pretty soon Freddy moved over to the other side of Jinx, so that people could see the fierce eyebrows and the terrifying moustache. The first person that got a good sight of Weedly was a little girl who was eating a lollipop. She had just pulled the stick out of the lollipop, in order to get more of the flavor, which was lemon, when she saw Weedly. She opened her eyes wide and drew in her breath sharply with fright, and the lollipop went with it. She began to make choking noises, and people rushed up and stood around and said, "Oh, Oh! The poor little thing!" But one man who knew what to do, picked her up and whacked her on the back, and the lollipop flew out and rolled off into the bushes. And the little girl went into the house crying, to ask her mother for some money to buy another lollipop.

That was bad enough, but the next person they met was a little old lady. Her name was Mrs. Peppercorn. Mrs. Peppercorn was nearly ninety. She had seen a lot of queer things, but in all her nearly ninety years she had never seen a pig with a black moustache and eyebrows. She was a very active old lady, and when she came face to face with Little Weedly she jumped right over Judge Willey's white picket fence.

Well, a number of things like this happened as they went along. Mr. Bickey, the coal man, fell right out of his front parlor window into a rosebush, which was not very pleasant for him, and Willis Fitts, who was repairing some stonework on the chimney of the First Presbyterian Church, gave a loud cry and disappeared down the chimney. Fortunately he stuck halfway down, so no bones were broken. But it took the Centerboro fire department three hours to get him out.

Little Weedly seemed rather pleased at these various demonstrations, and even began to strut a little. But when two automobile drivers had run their cars right up on the pavement in their panic, Jinx said: "If we go over to the movie theatre now, there'll be a riot. Couldn't I take him somewhere until after dark, and then slip in without being seen?"

Freddy suggested the jail, so they turned up

a side street and presently came to a large, pleasant looking house, sitting back from the sidewalk, and surrounded by green lawns bordered with flower beds. Little tables with gaily striped umbrellas over them stood about, and at them sat the prisoners, talking and playing games. There were open boxes of candy on nearly all the tables, and at one, an ice cream freezer was being opened. In the middle of the lawn, several prisoners were planting red geraniums in a large flower bed. They were working very fast, because the flower bed was to be a surprise for the sheriff. They were arranging the flowers to spell out the motto: THERE IS NO PLACE LIKE JAIL.

The animals went around to the back, where they found the sheriff refereeing a game of croquet.

"Sure," he said when Freddy had explained, "sure. Go right into the living room. There's nobody there now. Great potatoes, he *is* a tough looking customer, isn't he?"

So Jinx and Little Weedly waited at the jail, and Freddy went on down to the movies. When he got there a lot of people were going in and he paid his ten cents and went along in with them. It was dark inside, because the newsreel had started, and he slid into a seat about halfway down and folded his fore-trotters on his stomach and prepared to enjoy himself. He sat through the news and a cartoon, and a travel picture and the feature had begun and he was just wondering if Jinx and Weedly had got there yet, when a woman sat down in the seat next to him.

At first she didn't notice that she was sitting next to a pig. But pretty soon she turned and saw him. She jumped up and called in a loud voice: "Usher! Usher!"

People all around them turned and stared and said: "Hush! Sit down!" But the woman just shouted: "Send an usher down here!" And then she turned and pointed to Freddy. "I demand that this animal be removed!" she said. Then Freddy saw that it was Aunt Effie.

Uncle Snedeker, who sat on the other side of Aunt Effie, with his big hat on his knees, tugged at her shawl. "Eh, Effie, don't make a fuss," he whispered. "Here now; I'll change seats with you, eh? Lordy, I've sat next to pigs often enough in my life, I guess."

"If I thought you meant what I think you meant, Snedeker," she said, turning on him, "I'd—"

"No, no," he said, "I just meant— Eh, skip it. Come on, change seats. Don't spoil the show for everybody."

The audience were now nearly all on their feet, trying to see what the disturbance was about. "Put her out! We came here to see the show," someone in the back shouted. Freddy, who didn't want to make any trouble, started to get up and change his seat, but a man behind him put his hands on the pig's shoulders and pushed him down. "No you don't, Freddy," he said. "You've got as good a right here as she has, and there isn't anybody in Centerboro that wouldn't be proud to sit next to any of Mr. Bean's animals."

By this time the theatre was in an uproar. The picture stopped running, and the lights went up, and Mr. Muszkiski came waddling down the aisle. "What's all this—what's all this, madam?" he panted. He was a very fat man, and he always panted, even when he hadn't been running.

Aunt Effie stood up very straight and tall. Her shawl was pulled tight around her, and her bonnet nodded at Mr. Muszkiski as she pointed a long finger at Freddy and said: "I demand that this animal be removed."

"Yes, madam," said Mr. Muszkiski. Why?"

"Why?" snapped Aunt Effie. "Why?" She drew her lips into a tight line. "A pig!"

Mr. Muszkiski shook his head. "We make no class distinctions in this theatre, madam," he said. "Bankers, working men, Eskimos, Hottentots, elephants, lizards—we treat them all alike. If they have the price of admission, we let them in." He turned to Freddy. "You paid for your ticket, I suppose, sir?"

"Sure I did," said the pig. "But I don't want to make you any trouble, and if this lady insists—" but he didn't finish, for at his first word, Aunt Effie had fallen back into her seat.

"You—you can talk!" she gasped.

"Yes, madam, I can talk," said Freddy, very dignified.

"Eh, Effie, what did I tell you?" said Uncle

Snedeker. "You know what the sheriff said. Talking animals, eh? Well . . . What's that?" he said sharply. For a sudden babble of voices had arisen in the back of the theater, and as they tried to see what it was, they grew louder. There were cries of fright, and then a surge of people toward the door.

"What's the matter with them?" said Mr. Muszkiski, who had climbed on to a seat in order to see better. "Something's scared them. They'll be hurt.—Open the exits!" he shouted at the top of his lungs. "You—Jack! Open the doors!"

Uncle Snedeker crammed his hat on his head and seized Aunt Effie by the arm. "It's the Indians!" he shouted. "Eh, Effie, come along! They've set fire to the theatre. We must escape!"

Aunt Effie was too amazed at discovering that Freddy could talk, to protest. Besides, most of the audience, without knowing what had happened, had become panic-stricken and were pouring towards the exit. She turned her back on Freddy and pushed out into the aisle.

"It can't be a fire," said Freddy to himself,

"or I'd hear the fire engines. And if it should be Indians, I'd rather take my chance with them than get kicked and stepped on by that mob in the aisles." So he sat down in his seat again. In a few minutes the theater was empty. Only Mr. Muszkiski was left, still standing on a seat and trying to see what had caused the excitement.

And after a minute he saw. For out from under a seat came Jinx and Little Weedly.

"Wow!" yelled Mr. Muszkiski and he made a dash down to a little door to the right of the stage and waddled through and slammed it behind him.

"Hi, Freddy," said Jinx. "Well, I guess the show's over. Going home?"

"I guess so," said Freddy. "What started the riot? Was it—was it this?" and he pointed to Weedly.

"Yeah," said the cat. "I tried to make him keep down in his seat when the lights went up, but he heard your voice and stood up on his hind legs, and some of the folks saw him."

"I scared 'em good, Cousin Frederick," said Little Weedly happily.

"Yes. You probably scared 'em so good

they won't let us come to the movies any more. Well, let's go home.''

The street was full of people when they came out, but the lights in front of the theater had been turned out, and they managed to get out without attracting any attention. Once away from the theater, there was only a scattering of people, and most of them were running toward the theater to see what was going on. No one noticed them. Weedly had never been in a town before and he was very much interested in all the sights, particularly the colored lights in the drugstore window. He stopped to look at them. Suddenly he gave a jump and a squeal, and then tried to crawl under Jinx. "Oh, Uncle Jinx," he whispered, "what was that terrible animal? Oh, I want to go home!"

"Terrible animal?" said Freddy looking in the window and catching sight of his own pleasant face in a mirror, "I don't see any— oh, yes," he said, "I know what you saw. Here, Weedly—look." And he pulled him up to the window again.

Weedly trembled, but he did look again,

and there beside the dreadful face that had frightened him was the face of his cousin. And on the other side of it, Jinx appeared.

They had some trouble explaining to him what a mirror was, and how it worked, but when he saw that if he wiggled his nose or smiled, the terrible face did the same thing, he was convinced. He was rather pleased, too. "I look nice," he said. "I thought I looked like Cousin Frederick."

"Ha, that's one for you, Freddy," said Jinx.

"Oh," said Weedly, "I don't mean that Cousin Frederick isn't nice looking, but I think I look sort of stern and noble and—"

"Yeah, you look lovely," said Jinx impatiently. "But we can't stand here all night while you admire yourself. Come on home. I promise you that you'll look a lot more like your Cousin Frederick in the morning. Eh, Freddy?"

"You bet," said the pig. "We can't have him starting any more riots."

Chapter 7

After Aunt Effie took the teapot down and put it on the tea table in the parlor, the Webbs moved downstairs, and took up a temporary residence back of a framed steel engraving of Washington Crossing the Delaware, which hung between the front parlor windows. Here they could keep an eye on the teapot. The only difficulty was—how could they get word out quickly to the animals, if something important happened? Even when the grass outside was dry, it took a long time to get to

116

the barn or the pigpen. If the Snedekers decided to leave suddenly, they would be packed
up and gone before Mr. Webb could let the
animals know.

At last, however, they thought of a way.
There were no mouse-holes in the parlor, but
there was a way by which the mice could get
in through the cellar to the space under the
parlor floor. The Webbs talked it over with
the mice, and the mice agreed that one of
them would always be on duty under the floor.
Then if anything serious happened, Mr.
Webb could drop down the wall, slip through
a crack under the baseboard, jump on to the
mouse's back, and gallop off to warn the animals. It was a good arrangement, and it made
the Webbs feel quite important. It was almost
like having a private car and a chauffeur
always ready to take them wherever they
wanted to go.

On the morning after the riot in the movie
theater, Uncle Snedeker hitched up Hank to
the hay wagon and went out to bring in the
hay Aunt Effie had cut and raked the day before. A little while later, Mr. Webb kissed

Mrs. Webb goodby, and started off as usual for the cowbarn. "I don't suppose anything will happen while I'm away," he said, "but if it does, Cousin Augustus is on duty this morning, and he'll bring you down there in no time."

It was a fresh clear morning. Mr. Webb drew in deep breaths of the cool air as he strolled along through the grass and weeds that swayed in the breeze above his head. Pretty soon he heard someone singing, and then the song stopped and a thin voice called: "Hi, Webb!"

Mr. Webb looked up and saw a mosquito hanging to the under side of a burdock leaf.

"Morning, Jasper," he said. "Lovely day."

"Is it?" said the mosquito. "Say, look, Webb—when are the Beans coming home?"

"What's the matter?" Mr. Webb asked. "Do you miss the Beans, too?"

"Why wouldn't I miss 'em?" demanded Jasper. "I can't get a square meal in this place any more. You know that hole in the screen in the bedroom window? Well, I buzzed in

there last night and scouted around for a
while. Uncle Snedeker sleeps with the bedclothes over his head; there was no use tack-
ling him. So I lit on Aunt Effie's ear. Gosh, I
hardly touched it—you know how light I am
on my feet, Webb. And then—wham! Up
came her hand and missed me by—well, I'd
hate to tell you how little she missed me by.
Then she got up and lit the light and chased
me with a fly swatter. Believe me, I was glad
to get out of there!"

"I should think so, indeed," said Mr. Webb
sympathetically.

"Yes, *sir*," said the mosquito. " 'Tisn't like
the old days. Why, the Beans never minded a
mosquito bite or two—as long as we didn't
overdo it, of course."

They talked a few minutes longer, and then
Mr. Webb went on. He met a beetle he knew,
and several other acquaintances, and then just
as he was crossing the corner of the garden he
saw a strange caterpillar. The caterpillar was
eating a beet leaf, and he looked up at Mr.
Webb and winked, and then went on eating.

"Here, you!" said Mr. Webb sharply. "Just a minute! Do you know whose garden this is?"

"Sure—old Bean's," said the caterpillar, with his mouth full. "What of it?"

"There's this of it," said Mr. Webb angrily: "it's a private garden and no trespassers allowed. Now get out!"

"Oh, yeah?" said the caterpillar. And he was going to say more, but Mr. Webb, who was, like most spiders, rather short-tempered, rushed at him and nipped one of his legs.

"Ouch!" yelled the caterpillar. "Quit that, you big bully." He dropped off the leaf and curled up tightly with all his legs inside, and only his furry back exposed. "You wait," he mumbled. "We'll fix your old garden for you."

Mr. Webb couldn't bite through the caterpillar's fur, but one thing he could do, and that was tie the creature up so he couldn't move. But it was rather a long job, and he didn't want to take the time.

"I'll let you go this time," he said, "if you'll get out of here quick. Come on; get going!"

"Stop!" shouted Mr. Webb.

The caterpillar jumped up and dashed off. He was pretty scared, and kept trying to look back over his shoulder, with the result that his rear end went faster than his front end. He would begin to hump up in the middle and then turn a complete somersault. This made Mr. Webb laugh, but after a minute something the caterpillar had said made him frown thoughtfully, so he started after the intruder.

He walked down through the beet rows to the far end of the garden. He passed one or two other caterpillars, but didn't say anything to them. When he got there, he climbed on a fence post and looked out across the fields. As far as the eye could see—at least, a spider's eye, which can only see a few yards—stretched rank upon rank of caterpillars; regiment after regiment, with their leaders out in front, standing at ease, apparently awaiting word from their scouts, a number of whom were now hurrying back to report.

It must have been rather a terrifying sight for one small spider, but Mr. Webb did not hesitate. He scrambled down from the post and ran out to where, in front of the army, a little group of somewhat larger caterpillars, with gold stripes on their heads, were holding a conference. "Stop!" shouted Mr. Webb. "You can't come any farther."

The caterpillars laughed, and one, whom he took to be the leader, came forward. He looked Mr. Webb up and down, and then he said shortly: "Why?"

"It's Mr. Bean's garden," said the spider, "and caterpillars aren't allowed."

"Ha!" said the head caterpillar, turning to the members of his staff. "You hear that? Caterpillars not allowed. Give the order to advance!"

At once, several of the others reared up and swayed the upper parts of their bodies back and forth. The motion was taken up by the officers all along the line, and then the whole army surged forward toward Mr. Webb.

Mr. Webb said afterward that the thunder of their marching feet shook the very ground. Caterpillars have a good many extra feet but I think perhaps he exaggerated a little in this. Of course he was in a pretty dangerous spot. He couldn't decide whether to stay and sell his life as dearly as possible, or to run away and warn the animals. But at last he decided to postpone the decision. He would go see if Freddy could think of something. He could come back later and fight, if he wanted to.

The pigpen was not far away, and in a few minutes Mr. Webb was walking up and down the outside of the window beside Freddy's desk. Although the window was pretty dusty, he could dimly make out Freddy, sitting at the desk and he thought that this would be the quickest way to attract the pig's attention. And sure enough, after a minute Freddy looked up, and then he came running outside.

"Hello, Webb," he said; "I thought it was you. What's wrong?"

"Caterpillars," panted the spider. "Chewing up the garden. There won't be a leaf left by night if we don't do something."

"Gosh," said Freddy, "that's bad. I wish Mr. Bean was here. The only way to stop 'em is to dig a trench across their line of march, and then pour kerosene in and set fire to it. We animals can't do that. Well, I'll have to go see Aunt Effie. No time to write her another note. I'll have to go right up to the house." He sighed and shook his head dismally. "I'd rather face a den of rattlesnakes than that broom."

Chapter 8

Aunt Effie hadn't slept very well that night. First, there had been the mosquito, and then there had been a lot of troublesome thoughts arising out of what had happened at the movie theater. She had been within her rights in demanding that the pig be removed. Nobody would care to have the seat next her occupied by a pig. But the manager had refused to put him out, and the audience had backed him up. It was disgraceful!

The pig had acted well, too. He had not tried to stand on what he evidently thought were *his* rights. He had been quite gentlemanly, preferring to leave quietly rather than cause a disturbance. Somehow Aunt Effie felt that she had not come out of the encounter very well.

And then the discovery that the pig could talk! That was more disquieting than anything that had happened to her in a long time. She didn't really believe it, of course; she couldn't make herself believe it. And yet, if it hadn't been the pig who spoke, who was it?

She worried all night about these things, and at breakfast she was as cross as two sticks. Uncle Snedeker wanted to talk about what had happened at the theatre, which was quite natural, for if you have really heard an animal say something it makes a good topic of conversation. But Aunt Effie was pretty short with him.

"I do not care to discuss the matter," she said. "If you wish to talk to pigs you are of course free to do so, but I don't wish to hear about it."

"Eh, but it was you that talked to the pig, Effie, not me," he protested.

"We will not discuss it," said Aunt Effie. "Snedeker, take your elbows off the table!"

"Eh, I'm sorry, Effie, I'm sorry," said Uncle Snedeker, hastily drawing back his arms from the cloth. Uncle Snedeker's manners were usually almost perfect, thanks to Aunt Effie's training, but once in a while he would forget. It was an unlucky thing for him if he forgot when Aunt Effie happened to be sewing, because then she would rap his head with her thimble, and as he didn't have much hair, it hurt. This morning she was across the table, so all she could do was glare at him.

Nobody likes to be glared at, particularly when he is eating. Uncle Snedeker got nervous and choked on his coffee, and then he said: "Excuse me," and rose and went out to get the hay in.

When Aunt Effie had washed up the breakfast dishes, she went into the parlor and sat down in a chair to admire the silver teapot. It was a beautiful teapot. But what good was the most beautiful teapot if there was no one to give tea parties to? "No one but pigs!" she said bitterly. "Talking pigs!"

And at that moment there was a rap at the kitchen door, and she went and opened it and there stood Freddy.

"Excuse me, ma'am," he said quickly, "but there's trouble in the garden, and we thought you ought to know."

Aunt Effie couldn't seem to find her voice. She just stared.

Freddy explained. And at once Aunt Effie leaped to action. She didn't even wait to put on her bonnet. She got a hoe and the kerosene can from the woodshed and started for the garden. "Go get Snedeker," she called over her shoulder.

When Freddy and Uncle Snedeker reached the garden the battle was on in earnest. The beets had already been eaten right down to the ground, and the caterpillars had started on the beans. And in the little space between the first two bean rows, Aunt Effie and Robert and Georgie and the three cows were digging away with hoe and hoofs and paws. Pretty soon they had a trench dug, and Aunt Effie poured kerosene in and lit it. More animals were coming up all the time, but there wasn't much they could do to help. If they attacked the invaders, they would do more harm than good by trampling down the beans. They stood around in helpful attitudes, and watched the smoky flames run along the trench.

Caterpillars are not very bright, and usually if there is anything between them and what they have decided to eat, they will keep on marching right through it. If it is a trench full of fire they keep on until they are all burnt up. But these caterpillars were better trained. They had learned to obey orders, which is an important thing for anybody to learn, whether he is a caterpillar or a human. So when the officers ran rippling up and down the edge of the trench, shouting: "Column right—march!" the whole army turned as one cater-pillar and rolled up along the trench. And in a few minutes they had turned the end of it and were in among the beans and the lettuce and the tomatoes on the other side.

"Another trench!" shouted Aunt Effie,

swinging her hoe. "Come along, you animals!" She realized that by the time the other trench was dug it would be too late. Already a dozen of the best tomato plants had been captured, and squads of hungry caterpillars were pushing in among the young corn. But she was not one to give up easily, and the animals followed her willingly.

In the meantime, Mr. Webb, unwilling to remain in idleness when there were deeds to be done, had returned to the battlefield. Not that any deeds he could do would make much difference in the outcome. A few caterpillars tied up and helpless wouldn't save the garden. But he had an idea. He reached the trench just as the caterpillars abandoned the attempt to storm it and turned to outflank it. He dashed down the bean rows, peering through the smoke that almost stifled him. Now and then a flame, blown by the wind, licked toward him, and he darted back to avoid being burnt. But fortune favors the bold. Standing on a stone and surveying the operations with a satisfied smile, was the head caterpillar.

Mr. Webb also smiled a satisfied smile.

Quickly he spun a strand of web, and holding it in his mouth he crept up behind the caterpillar. When he was close enough he jumped, and bit the caterpillar in his third right hind leg, at the same time slipping the loop around it. The caterpillar reared up and half turned around, and Mr. Webb pulled the loop around his first left front leg, quickly jerked it tight, and fastened it. Then he rolled the helpless caterpillar off the stone and after tying a few more of his legs together, hid him under a plantain leaf. "There," he said, "I guess nobody will rescue you for a while."

Although the caterpillars were deprived of a leader, and although the second trench was nearly dug, so many of them were now in the garden that there was little hope of saving it. Caterpillars are fortunate in one respect; they can eat twenty-four hours a day without ever getting a stomach-ache. And so, although they are small, they eat a great deal. The garden was just disappearing.

As Mr. Webb came out after hiding the leader, he saw that there was some commotion among the caterpillars. Many of them had

. . . slipping the loop around it.

stopped eating and were staring with lifted heads toward a corner of the garden. One whole regiment, who were now advancing on the cabbages had stopped, and seemed to be thrown into confusion. Mr. Webb climbed up a tomato vine and joined a group of them to see what they were looking at.

"Hey, spider," said one of the caterpillars, "what kind of an animal is that?" He nodded his head toward a clump of bushes at the edge of the garden, from which a head was peering out.

It was a pretty queer kind of a head. Mr. Webb had never seen anything like it before. It looked like a pig, but it had fierce black moustaches and scowling black eyebrows. It was, of course, Little Weedly, though Mr. Webb didn't know that. What he did know, though, was that here was a chance to give the caterpillars a good scare.

"Wow!" he said. "You boys better go while the going's good."

"What do you mean?" said the caterpillar.

"Just what I say. He eats caterpillars."

"Go on!" said the caterpillar. "Are you

trying to kid me or something? There aren't any animals that eat caterpillars."

"Is that so!" said Mr. Webb. "Well, of course, maybe you know best. Go ahead, boys. Tuck into your dinner. Maybe it's the last one you'll eat, so don't waste time talking."

This seemed to make the caterpillar nervous. "But there aren't, I tell you," he insisted. "I guess I ought to know."

"You ought to," said the spider, "but you don't. Remember that circus that was here last year? No, I guess you don't; you weren't around here then. Anyway, they had this animal in a cage—at least, I suppose it's the same animal, for he was the only one in captivity. He must have escaped. I did hear yesterday that some of their animals escaped."

"Yes, yes," interrupted the caterpillar impatiently, "but what *is* he?"

"Oh, didn't I tell you? The Greater Siberian Caterpillar-Eater. Yes, sir; that's what they called him. Eats nothing but caterpillars —all kinds. People came from miles around to see him, and some of them— Hey, where

you going?" he called, for the caterpillar and
his friends had dropped to the ground and
were making off as fast as they could go.

In five minutes word had gone through the
entire army that a Greater Siberian Caterpillar-Eater was at large and about to attack
them. None of the caterpillars had ever heard
of such an animal, but that made him even
more terrible to them, and as each one added
something to the story as he passed it on, in
no time at all the whole army, with no leader
to rally them, was in a panic-stricken retreat.

"H'm," said Mr. Webb to himself, "I expect it would be sort of a joke on me if he
turned out to be a Greater Siberian Spider-
Eater. I wonder what he really is?" And
then Little Weedly came out of the bushes
with Jinx beside him. "Why, it's that
Weedly!" said the spider. "Who on earth
painted him up like that? Well, I guess I'd
better go back and tell mother about the excitement. She'll be wild, not being in on it."

Chapter 9

Freddy had helped in the digging of the second trench, and was watching Aunt Effie set fire to the kerosene. There was something, he kept thinking—something important that he ought to remember. Something he had seen that day,—what on earth was it? If he could only remember it, he knew somehow that it was of the utmost importance to every animal on the farm.

He looked around. Uncle Snedeker and

the cows and the dogs and a whole crowd of smaller animals were standing in a big half-circle, looking on. "Every last one of them has his mouth open," he thought. "I wonder why people can't seem to look at a fire without having their mouths open. Open!" he exclaimed suddenly. "That's it! The back door is open. Aunt Effie left it that way in her hurry." He turned and ran for the house.

The kitchen door was wide. Freddy dashed through, across the kitchen and down the hall to the parlor door. But the parlor door was shut.

It isn't an easy thing for a pig to turn a door-knob, particularly a slippery white china one. Freddy could get it in his mouth all right, but turning it was something else again. "Patience," he said to himself. "Patience. The more haste the less speed, old boy. Anyway, she'll be busy for a couple of hours with those caterpillars." And finally he got it.

And there glittered the teapot among the tea things on the little table by the window.

Freddy should have seized the teapot and made off with it without a moment's delay.

But he was a poet as well as a pig of action. It was very quiet and cozy in the parlor, with the chairs pulled up about the teatable, and the large framed photographs of Mrs. Bean's father and mother looking down from the wall. Freddy was no greedier than most pigs, but he thought how nice it would be to have tea in this pleasant room, with little cakes and sandwiches and tea biscuit and buttered muffins and doughnuts and perhaps a few candies and possibly ice cream to follow. He sat down in a deep red plush chair and pretended that he was a guest at such a teaparty, and then he began to make up a poem about it.

> *When day is done and shadows creep*
> *Across the lawn, then set to steep*
> *The teapot on the table-top*
> *And lay aside the broom and mop*
> *And pile the plates with little cakes*
> *Nor think at all of stomach aches,*
> *But gather round and fill your cups*
> *And—*

He had got as far as this when his eye, rolling in poetic frenzy, rested for a moment on

George Washington Crossing the Delaware, and on the corner of the frame he saw Mrs. Webb waving frantically to him.

"Pups," he said, "—no, that won't do. Hiccoughs? No, no,—what is it, Mrs. Webb?"

He couldn't hear what she was saying, but there was no mistaking the urgency of her gestures. She wanted him to hurry, to take the teapot and run. Well, perhaps she was right. She didn't know how busy Aunt Effie was going to be for the next hour or so, of course, but perhaps it really was the sensible thing to get the teapot into safety first. He put his foretrotters on the table, seized the spout of the teapot in his mouth, and started out of the door.

And ran straight into Aunt Effie.

"Well, well," said Aunt Effie, closing the door and putting her back to it. "Put the teapot down, please," she said quietly.

So Freddy put it down and she picked it up, wiped it on her apron, and set it back on the table. Then she said: "Sit down: I want to talk to you."

Freddy sat down on a little ottoman covered with carpet which had a pattern of red roses on a pink background. He looked, and felt, very uncomfortable, partly, of course, because he had been caught, but partly, too, because he knew that pink wasn't his color. It made him look very fat.

Aunt Effie sat down by the teatable and rested her elbow on it, and put her forefinger against her head. "I have never liked animals very well," she said. "Especially pigs. They have no manners, and I have always found that people who have no manners can't be trusted."

"Excuse me, ma'am," said Freddy, "but I think you can't have known very many animals or you wouldn't say that." And he blushed bright pink, which was very becoming to him, because it made him more nearly the color of the ottoman. But of course he didn't know that.

"Please let me finish," said Aunt Effie. "Last night I refused to sit next you in the theatre. I am bound to admit that you acted very well about it. I found that though you could talk, you didn't say anything, which seemed to me truly remarkable. I do not change my mind readily, but I began to think that maybe I had been wrong,—not about all animals, but about you."

"The other animals on this farm are no different than I am," said Freddy.

"Perhaps not," said Aunt Effie. "But it was not the other animals who warned me about the garden this morning. It was you, and it was a very friendly act. At least so I supposed. But now I find you in here stealing my teapot."

"It's not your teapot," said Freddy bluntly, "it's Mrs. Bean's."

"It's in Mrs. Bean's house, but it is *not* Mrs. Bean's teapot," said Aunt Effie. "It belonged to my mother, Mr. Bean's grandmother. It was supposed to be left to me.—But I don't know why I should explain all this to a pig. Even a very exceptional pig."

"You might have to explain it to a policeman," said Freddy.

Aunt Effie sat up very straight. "See here," she said, "do you mean to accuse me of being a thief?"

"No," said Freddy. "No, not exactly. I think you *think* the teapot should be yours. But then why don't you ask Mrs. Bean for it when she's home? I know Mrs. Bean, and I know she wouldn't keep anything that didn't belong to her—not for two minutes."

"Bah!" said Aunt Effie explosively. "She's kept it ten years."

"Then it belongs to her," said Freddy firmly. "And I might as well tell you, Mrs. Snedeker—" He stopped, for the door had opened and Uncle Snedeker came into the room.

"Eh!" said Uncle Snedeker. "Well, pickle me and preserve me if it isn't the talking pig! So you talk, eh? Hold conversations and make speeches and all. Eh? Come, speak up. If you can talk, why don't you do it, eh?"

"Be quiet, Snedeker, and sit down," snapped Aunt Effie. "How can he talk when you gabble all the time? Go on," she said to Freddy.

"I was only going to say," said the pig, "that we animals aren't going to let you leave here with that teapot. If you want to stay and look after the farm until the Beans come home, that's all right with us. But if you try to take the teapot away—well, we just won't let you do it, that's all."

"Ha!" said Uncle Snedeker. "Very high and mighty, aren't you, pig? Telling us what we can and can't do, eh? Telling us—"

"Oh, shut *up*, Snedeker," said Aunt Effie exasperatedly. And then to Freddy: "May I ask how you intend to stop us?"

Freddy hadn't the slightest idea, and he began to wonder if he hadn't said too much. If they should suddenly decide to go now . . .

"The sheriff is a very good friend of ours," he said.

"The sheriff!" said Aunt Effie. "Dear me, I wouldn't count on him too much if I were you. He would hardly believe your word against mine. He has been most helpful since we have been here. He wrote me such a nice note about the hay."

"Signed it 'An Admirer'," put in Uncle Snedeker triumphantly. "I guess that surprises you, eh? I guess you won't get much help from him."

"Why, he ain't a lady."

"The sheriff didn't write that note," said Freddy. "I did. On my typewriter."

"Well, tear off my collar and necktie!" Uncle Snedeker began, but Aunt Effie interrupted him.

"I will *not* have this dreadful swearing, Snedeker," she said. "Remember, there are ladies present."

"Why, he ain't a lady," said Uncle Snedeker, pointing at Freddy.

"And don't point," said Aunt Effie. "No," she said, "but I am, I hope?"

"Eh, yes, yes, I see what you mean," said Uncle Snedeker, and subsided.

Aunt Effie turned again to Freddy. "Will you explain," she said, "just why, if you wrote that note, you signed it in the way you did?" She looked at him almost pleasantly, and he was both surprised and relieved, for he had expected that she would fly into a rage. But he didn't, of course, know that for all the nice teaparties she gave back in Orenville, nobody had ever said that he admired her before.

"Well," he said, "I expect you won't believe me, but I signed it that way because I—

well, I really do admire you."

"Eh, dry-clean my Sunday vest!" said Uncle Snedeker under his breath.

Aunt Effie was still looking expectantly at Freddy, and in spite of his embarrassment, he had to go on.

"I thought it was very good of you to do so much work around the farm just to keep it running properly. And then—well, I like teaparties pretty well myself."

"You like teaparties!" said Aunt Effie, looking at him now almost kindly. "What a pity that there is no way for animals to give them."

"Mrs. Bean sometimes gives teaparties *for* the animals," said Freddy.

"Well, curl my eyewinkers!" said Uncle Snedeker. "Do you propose that Aunt Effie—?"

"No, no," said Freddy quickly. "She wouldn't want to give us a party when we think she's taking something that doesn't belong to her." He stopped a minute, looking up at Washington Crossing the Delaware. There was Mrs. Webb, listening to every word, and as he looked up she waved at him.

He had just thought of a way, if he could work it, of keeping the Snedekers at the farm a few days longer. "And about the teapot," he said, "if you did try to go away with it, we'd tell the sheriff. And if you stay here and hide it— well, you couldn't possibly hide it where we couldn't find it. Why, I'll prove it to you. When I'm gone, you hide it somewhere—any-where in the house or barn or outside, only of course you mustn't take it away. And I'll come back tomorrow this time and tell you where you hid it. I won't hunt around for it— I'll just tell you."

"Hey!" said Uncle Snedeker leaning for-ward. "That's a good one, that is. Eh, Effie? Mind-reader, hey?" He put one hand behind his back. "Maybe you can tell me how many fingers I'm holding out, eh?"

Freddy looked up at Washington Crossing the Delaware. Mrs. Webb was holding up three legs. Freddy said: "Three."

"Eh!" shouted Uncle Snedeker. "He's right, Effie! Why, he is a mind-reader. He read my mind like an open book."

"Don't be ridiculous, Snedeker," said Aunt

Effie. "He couldn't read your mind. You have to *have* a mind before anyone can read it. It was just guesswork."

"I guessed right, though," said the pig. "And I can guess right with the teapot. You try it."

"Very well, I will," said Aunt Effie. "And if you can find it—"

"If I can find it," Freddy interrupted, "you'll promise to stay here until the Beans get home and ask Mrs. Bean if she'll give you the teapot."

"Oh, no," said Aunt Effie. "I won't do that. I don't have to make any promises. Not that I think you can find the teapot, but you might happen to guess right. No," she said, "but I tell you what I *will* do." And she smiled at Freddy, which surprised Uncle Snedeker so that he nearly fell off his chair. "I'll give you animals the best teaparty you ever had."

"Will you really?" exclaimed Freddy. "That would be wonderful."

"Eh, look out, Effie," said Uncle Snedeker. "You get all those animals in here and they'll just grab the teapot and run off with it."

"No, we won't, either," said the pig. "I give you warning that after the teaparty's over, we'll try to get it, because we don't think you have any right to it. But just because we disagree on that one point, doesn't mean that we can't forget our differences for one afternoon. Anyway, it wouldn't be very polite to do anything like that. There isn't one of the animals, Mrs. Snedeker, who will as much as mention the teapot at your party."

"Eh, well," said Uncle Snedeker, "I don't see why you'd come to the teaparty anyway. If I didn't like people, I wouldn't accept their invitations."

"We didn't like you when you came," said Freddy. "And we still don't like your trying to get the teapot. But you've fought the caterpillars and done a lot of things for us, and to keep the farm going, and we like you for that. We'll fight you for the teapot if we have to, but in the meantime I don't see why we can't be pleasant about it."

"Well, that's settled then," said Aunt Effie. "You better go on back to your haying, Snedeker. And you, er—Freddy, is that your name? —you run along now and come back tomorrow at this time and tell me where the teapot is hidden."

"I don't get you, pig," said Uncle Snedeker as he and Freddy went across the barnyard together. "Eh, I expect you're just trying to throw us off our guard, pretending to like us."

"I told you that I admired Mrs. Snedeker," said Freddy, "and that's true."

"Well, maybe," said Uncle Snedeker doubtfully.

"And as Mrs. Snedeker enjoys giving tea-parties, and as we enjoy going to them, why shouldn't we all be polite to one another for an afternoon?"

"Eh, I dunno," said Uncle Snedeker. "Effie's great on politeness. I don't say I dislike it myself. In other people, that is. It's kind of an effort for me to be polite. I guess maybe I wasn't brought up right."

"Why, I think you're polite all right," said Freddy.

"Eh, there you go. Now you're just *being* polite," said Uncle Snedeker.

"You're getting me all mixed up," said Freddy. "Honestly, I think you're polite."

"Eh, well," Uncle Snedeker sighed. "I suppose you don't admire me especially?" he asked. "Just a teeny bit, eh?"

Freddy looked thoughtful for a minute. "Well," he said, "you remind me a good deal of a circus lion who's a great friend of mine. The things you say. He's always saying, 'Well, dye my hair!' and things like that."

Uncle Snedeker was greatly pleased. "Remind you of a lion, eh? Well, that's admiration if anything is. A lion. Big, strong, ferocious beasts—"

"Snedeker!" came Aunt Effie's voice from the door. "Go get that hay in!"

"Going, Effie. Going," said Uncle Snedeker and scuttled off.

"So, he's like a lion, is he?" said Jinx, coming around the corner of the barn. "Reminds me more of a mouse. What's been going on, Freddy?"

The pig told him. But Jinx wasn't pleased.

"Teaparty indeed!" he said. "What do we want a teaparty for? You weren't very smart,

Freddy, telling her that we liked her. I don't like that woman and never will."

"Well, I don't know," said Freddy. "I do admire her, as I told you. And honestly, I'm beginning to kind of like her. Oh, I know she's trying to grab Mrs. Bean's teapot. But what's the harm of a party? It'll keep her here a couple more days, and then we can think of something else. And I don't believe she's ever had much fun. She loves to give tea-parties, and she's pretty unhappy here with nobody to give them to. What's the harm?"

"She must have buttered you up good to get you feeling so loving towards her," said Jinx. "Paid you a lot of compliments, I expect. You always were a sucker for compliments, Freddy."

"Well, she did say I was exceptional," said Freddy modestly. "But why are you so down on the party? Milk in little bowls—cream, maybe—and a sprig of catnip at every place—things like that. Only of course I suppose if you feel that way about her you won't go."

"Who says I won't go?" demanded Jinx. "If everybody else is going, I'm certainly not going to stay away. Only of course you've got to find the teapot after she hides it. I guess that'll give you something to think about. I guess I won't get dressed up for the party just yet."

"Pooh," said Freddy. "That's the easiest part of it."

Chapter 10

Freddy's study was a corner of the pigpen where he kept his books and his papers, and the disguises he used in his detective work, and his stamp collection. He had an old typewriter on a rickety desk and in front of it was an old easy chair which, if you sat down in it suddenly, puffed out clouds of dust that made you choke and sneeze. The whole place was terribly dusty, but although a number of his friends had offered to tidy it up for him,

Freddy wouldn't let them. "I like it this way," he said. "I'm naturally one of those very energetic people who wear themselves all out by working too hard and too fast. In here, now, I have to move slowly, because if I didn't I'd raise so much dust that I'd choke to death."

"But you might at least have the window washed," said Mrs. Wiggins one day. "Why, you can't even recognize your friends three feet away through that glass."

"That's just why I like it," said Freddy. "It gives me ideas when I'm sitting here working at my poetry. Everything outside looks a little different than what it is. When you go by, for instance, if the window was clean, why I'd just think: 'There goes Mrs. Wiggins,' and I'd remember a lot of things I wanted to tell you, and would forget all about my work. But if the window's dirty, I'd think: 'My goodness, what can that be? Is it an elephant?' And then I'd have something to write about."

But Mrs. Wiggins didn't understand what he was trying to say, and she said: "Well, if you write about me that I look like an elephant, Freddy, it'll be pretty mean of you,

that's all I can say. My land, I know I'm big
and clumsy, but I don't think it's nice of my
friends to make fun of me."

Freddy had quite a time explaining that
that wasn't what he had meant at all.

Today he was sitting at his typewriter,
pecking out the *Cast of Characters* for his
play. A few of the animals had told him what
parts they would like to take, and this is what
he already had down:

SHERLOCK HOLMES...Freddy

A G-MAN...............Jinx

QUEEN ELIZABETH...Mrs. Wiggins

CAPT. KIDD............Hank

Freddy was rather worried. A play has to
have at least one villain in it, and so far he had
nothing but heroes. He was wondering if he
could persuade the rooster to play the part of
the villain. If Charles was given a lot of
speeches to make, maybe he wouldn't mind
being villainous and being dragged off to jail,
or having his head chopped off in the last act.
Only, they would have to be pretty long

speeches, and when Charles got going he seldom stopped even after all the audience had left the hall.

There was a timid tap on the door, and when Freddy shouted: "Come in!", Alice and Emma, the two ducks, waddled into the pigpen.

"Good morning, Freddy," said Alice. "We heard about your play, and we thought we'd just stop in and see if you could possibly find any place in it for us."

"We'd love to be in it," said Emma. "And you know our Uncle Wesley always said that we were born actresses. I do think we might help to make it a success."

"I'm sure you would," said Freddy. "The main trouble now is that I haven't any villains. Of course everybody can choose what character he wants to play. I suppose you wouldn't want to take the parts of gangsters, would you?"

"We-ell," said Alice doubtfully, "we'd rather thought something more like Greta Garbo. Or maybe Norma Shearer. I don't know. Though Emma can look awfully wicked. Emma, make that tiger face for Freddy."

So Emma stuck her head forward and squinted her eyes and glared at him. Like her sister, she was a fluffy little white duck, and she certainly didn't look much like a tiger, Freddy thought. She looked much more like a little white duck trying to look wicked and not succeeding very well. It was all he could do not to laugh.

"That's wonderful," he said. "It's really quite startling. Quite tigerish, in fact. But I'm not sure it wouldn't be better for you to take parts that are more like you really are. After all, we need some actors in the play who will be charming and graceful, and although you, Emma, can certainly look awfully villainous, I certainly would prefer to see you being your own delightful self on the stage. And you too, of course, Alice."

The ducks looked at each other happily, and Alice tittered slightly. "Why, Freddy, that is a very nice compliment," she said. "Indeed I think perhaps you are right. Don't you, sister?"

"Yes," said Emma. "But I don't think just being ourselves is enough. I mean, it wouldn't be really acting, would it? I think we ought to have very sad parts, where we cry and carry on a lot—in a ladylike way, of course."

"Dear me, do you?" said Freddy. "Well, well, perhaps we could arrange it. Suppose you are Greta Garbo, Alice, and you, Emma, are Norma Shearer, and you are—let me see, ladies-in-waiting to Queen Elizabeth. That's Mrs. Wiggins, you know. Then I'll make up very sad parts for you."

The ducks thought that would be nice, and Freddy wrote it down: "Alice and Emma: two ladies-in-waiting, who have had a lot of trouble." Then he walked to the door with them, and stood looking after them as they waddled happily off toward the duck pond.

He had just started back to his work when he heard an excited quacking and fluttering, so he hurried to the door again. Alice and Emma, with their wings spread and their short little legs working like mad, were scooting up the lane towards home. "Hey, girls!"

"Boo!"

shouted Freddy. "What's the matter? Did something scare you?" But the ducks just went on, like clumsy little overloaded airplanes trying to get off the ground.

"They're having trouble already," said Freddy to himself. "Something must have scared them. Maybe a snake. I'd better go see."

So he went slowly across the barnyard to the corner of the fence. And just as he got there, something jumped out and said, "Boo!"

Afterwards Freddy said that the reason he jumped so high, and ran so fast when he came down, was that his legs were startled. "I wasn't really frightened," he said. "Not myself. Goodness, a little thing like that couldn't frighten me. But my legs were, I guess, and you know how it is when your legs start to go somewhere. It takes a few minutes to stop them." But whatever the cause of it was, Freddy was inside the pigpen with the door shut before his legs stopped going. "Whoosh!" he said, and sank into his chair.

But after a minute he got up and opened the door a crack and peeked out. "Good land!" he said. For Little Weedly was standing by the fence corner, grinning. He certainly didn't look very terrifying. Particularly as Jinx had washed his face that morning and the eyebrows and moustache were gone.

Freddy threw the door open. "Hey, you!" he said. "Weedly! Come here."

"Hello, Cousin Frederick," said Weedly, coming towards him. He walked with what was almost a swagger. "Scared you good, didn't I?"

"You come in here," said Freddy severely. "I want to talk to you."

Weedly stopped. "You're mad," he said. "I don't want to talk to you when you're mad."

"I'll be still madder if you don't come in here," said Freddy. So after a minute Weedly came in.

"I wasn't doing anything, Cousin Frederick," he said. "Just scaring a couple of old ducks! And then when you came along, I thought I'd try it on you. Golly, I didn't suppose *you'd* be so scared!"

"I was *not* frightened," said Freddy firmly.

"What did you run for?" Weedly asked.

"I just remembered that I had left the—ah, the door open. But we are not talking about me. Please stick to the point. Alice and Emma are kind and gentle, and they're very much smaller than you. You might have made them quite ill, scaring them like that."

"Pooh," said Weedly, "they'll get over it. Besides, Mrs. Wiggins isn't smaller than I am, and I scared her good this morning." He began to giggle. "Gosh, Cousin Frederick, these animals around here are a scary lot, aren't they? I should think they'd get over it after a while. I used to be scary too, remember?"

"I wish we'd let you stay that way," said Freddy. "My goodness, Weedly, it isn't nice to go around scaring people. You won't be very popular if you keep it up."

"I wasn't very popular when I was so scary," said Weedly. "Anyway, it don't hurt 'em, and it's lots of fun."

"Well, I give you up," said Freddy. "Only, if some animal turns around and gives you a good licking some day, don't say I didn't tell you so."

"Pooh," said Weedly, "there isn't one of them that would dare."

"Is that so! Well—" Freddy hesitated a minute and then he said: "Well, don't try any of your tricks on Old Whibley, that's all."

"Who's Old Whibley?" Weedly asked. "A lion?"

"No. He's an owl who lives· up in the woods. You know what an owl is, don't you?"

"No, I don't," said Weedly. "Is he very big? —Not that I'm afraid of him, no matter how big he is," he added.

"He's a bird," said Freddy. "He lives in a big hollow maple that's to the right of the path, about halfway through the woods. He's not very big. But you take my advice and let him alone."

Little Weedly looked at him suspiciously. "Now you're trying to scare *me*, Cousin Frederick," he said. "But it won't work. I'm going right up to the woods now. My goodness, I'm not afraid of an old bird! Boy, won't I make that owl jump!" And he ran out of the door.

Freddy looked after him for a minute. "I

hope I haven't done wrong," he said. "Jinx will be mad as hops if Whibley really hurts him. But just the same, we can't have this kind of thing going on." And he went back to his desk.

He had been working for about half an hour, glancing up occasionally at the window with an expectant air, when at last he saw what he had been waiting for: the shadow of a spider walking up and down on the outside of the panes to attract his attention. He ran out quickly, and Mr. Webb hopped down onto his ear and said:

"It's all right, Freddy. As soon as you'd gone, Mrs. Webb climbed right down from the picture frame and into the spout of the teapot. She certainly got a nice long ride! First, Aunt Effie carried it down and hid it in the coalbin; then she took it upstairs and put it in one of Mr. Bean's rubber boots, and then she took it back down and hid it in Mrs. Bean's old sunbonnet that hangs behind the kitchen door. Then she started to bake a big batch of cookies. Mrs. Webb was going to get out then, because she thought I'd be worried not finding her when I got home, but she thought maybe she'd better wait a while, and it was a good thing she did, for when the cookies were done Aunt Effie put the teapot in the cake tin and piled cookies all over it and shut down the lid."

"My goodness," said Freddy, "that wasn't very nice for Mrs. Webb. How did she get out?"

"Well, she had quite a time. She said she pretty nearly smothered in that teapot with hot cookies piled all around it. She got out the spout and up through the cookies as fast as she could. But she had an awful time getting out of the cake tin. You know there are some small holes in the lid, but they'd be a tight squeeze even for an ant, and Mrs. Webb isn't as slender as she was. But she made it somehow, and got back to the picture frame all right."

"That's fine, Webb," said Freddy. "We certainly owe Mrs. Webb a vote of thanks. I hope she's feeling all right after such an experience."

"Yes," said the spider, "she had a good

night's sleep. And she doesn't want any thanks, you know. We'd do anything for the Beans."

"Well," said Freddy, "I guess I'd better go along up to the house and do my mind-reading stunt before Aunt Effie decides to hide the teapot somewhere else. Can I give you a lift?"

"No, I must get on down to the cowbarn." said Mr. Webb. "But there's one other thing you ought to know. Uncle Snedeker was trying last night to get Aunt Effie to tell him where she'd hidden the teapot. But she wouldn't. 'Why,' he said, 'you mean you don't trust me?' Aunt Effie said no, but he couldn't keep a secret. 'That pig's clever,' she said, 'and when he comes in here to find the teapot I'm not going to have you keep staring at the place where it's hidden. And you know,' she said, 'that's what you'd do.' Uncle Snedeker said: 'Pooh! that pig can't find it!' 'No,' Aunt Effie said, 'I know he can't.' And then after a minute she said: 'But you know what I'm going to do? I'm going to give them a teaparty anyway. I know how it is,' she said, 'to like teaparties and never be able to go to any, and so I'm going to give the animals one.'

"Well, then Uncle Snedeker said he thought maybe it was a good idea. 'Get the animals in a good humor,' he said, 'and maybe they'll let us have the teapot.' But Aunt Effie got quite cross at him. 'That isn't the idea at all,'' she said. 'I tell you, Snedeker,' she said, 'I didn't think anybody could teach me much about manners and politeness, but that pig has. He's taught me that you can be polite to people even when they're your enemies.' Uncle Snedeker said there wasn't anything in her etiquette book about that, he'd bet. Aunt Effie said well, there ought to be. And then Uncle Snedeker gave a kind of grunt and went off to bed.''

"H'm," said Freddy. "So she'll give us the party anyway. You know, that's kind of nice of her, Webb."

"Yes," said Mr. Webb, "I daresay. I'm not much for teaparties myself. But if a teaparty will keep her here a few days longer, I'm all for it. Well, so long, Freddy."

So Freddy went over to the house and

rapped on the kitchen door. After a minute Aunt Effie opened it. "Well, well; what do you want?" she demanded crossly, and then seeing who it was, her face changed and she smiled and said: "Oh, it's you, my young friend. Come in."

Uncle Snedeker was just coming up from the cellar with a scuttle of coal. "Eh, it's the talking pig!" he said. "Going to tell us where the teapot is. Eh, well, you can try. But you only get one guess, you understand."

"It isn't a guess," said Freddy. "I know where it is."

"Well, you're a smart pig if you do," said Aunt Effie, and Uncle Snedeker said: "Pooh, he couldn't guess it in a million years!"

"I told you how many fingers you were holding out yesterday, didn't I?"

"Just a lucky guess," said Uncle Snedeker. He set down the scuttle and put one hand behind him. "How many, now?" he said.

But Freddy didn't see Mrs. Webb anywhere in the kitchen, so he said loftily: "Oh, I haven't time for those little easy tricks now. I can tell you one thing, though. *You* don't know where the teapot is."

Uncle Snedeker looked surprised. "I don't, and that's a fact," he said.

"But I do," said Freddy. "It's covered up with cookies, in the cake tin, in the pantry."

"Well, my good gracious!" exclaimed Aunt Effie. "He's right, Snedeker." She went into the pantry and brought out the tin. "Though how he knew it, I can't imagine."

"Peekin'," said Uncle Snedeker. "That's what he was doing."

"No, he wasn't," said Aunt Effie. "He wasn't anywhere around, and neither were any of the other animals."

"Even if I had been peeking," said Freddy, "I couldn't have seen you hide it in the coal-bin, and then upstairs in Mr. Bean's boot, and then down here in Mrs. Bean's sunbonnet, before you put it in with the cookies."

"How on earth did you find out all that?" demanded Aunt Effie, staring at him in amazement. "Why it's—it's magic!"

"Well, ma'am," said Freddy, "I'd rather not tell you how I did it. Maybe I will some day. But I suppose we get our teaparty, don't we?"

"Yes," said Aunt Effie, "you do. Tomorrow afternoon. I'll give you the best teaparty you ever had. —Snedeker, get away from those cookies!" she said, turning quickly to slap Uncle Snedeker's wrist, which was just disappearing into the cake tin. "I'm keeping those for the party."

Uncle Snedeker retreated, grumbling, and Freddy said: "You know there are quite a lot of us. If you want any help—"

But Aunt Effie shook her head. "When I give a party," she said, "my guests are company. All they have to do is to come and have a good time."

"Have a good time!" grumbled Uncle Snedeker from the other side of the room. "A mob of animals! There'll be a lot of dishes broken, I bet. Eh, not that it matters much. They're the Beans' dishes."

"Well, naturally," said Aunt Effie, "we don't expect animals to have as good manners as people."

"Don't you worry, ma'am," said Freddy. "We'll all have our company manners on."

Chapter 11

Little Weedly trotted along up the bank of the brook towards the woods. "An old bird!" he said to himself. "As if I couldn't scare an old bird!" And he giggled.

Pretty soon he came to the duck pond. He thought he'd sneak up quietly behind a bush and if Alice and Emma were there, he could scare them again. And sure enough, there they were. But they were acting very queer. They were sitting on the bank, looking very sad, and first Alice would give a deep sigh and say: "Oh, deary, deary me!" and then Emma would give a deeper sigh and say: "Alas! Alackaday!" And then they would look at each other and sob.

Weedly watched them for a few minutes. Then he giggled. "My goodness!" he said. "When I scare 'em they certainly stay scared. I guess maybe I'd better not do it again." Then he began to feel sorry for them, because they seemed so terribly unhappy, so he crept backward out of the bush and then came walking along again towards the pond until they caught sight of him.

"Is there something the matter?" he said. "Are you in trouble?"

The ducks stopped sighing and looked up at him.

"It's that little pig that Jinx adopted," said Alice to her sister. "No," she said to Weedly, "we're just practicing being sad for the play Freddy is going to give. We're to have parts in it, you know. We're ladies-in-waiting to the queen, and we have a secret sorrow."

"My goodness, there isn't anything very

secret about it," said Weedly. "I should think if it was a *secret* sorrow you'd try to hide it. I should think you'd have to act very happy."

The ducks looked at each other. "Dear me," said Emma, "we didn't think of that, sister. I suppose we ought to act very gay. Like this." She gave a little quacking laugh, and then quickly turned her head aside as if to wipe away a tear.

"That's it, sister," said Alice. "That's it. A laugh that hides your breaking heart, and then to show that your heart really is breaking, under all your gaiety, you stop laughing and cry a little."

"Oh, yes, I think that is *much* more artistic," said Emma. Then suddenly she looked sharply at Weedly and said: "Why, you're the little wretch that jumped out and said 'Boo!' at us! I remember now."

"Well, yes," said Weedly. "I did. I scared you good, didn't I?" He tried to laugh, but the ducks were both looking at him now so ferociously that he thought he'd better not. "I—well I hope you aren't mad," he said, beginning to back away. "It was just in fun."

"In fun, was it?" said Emma. "Well, it wasn't fun for us, I can tell you. If our Uncle Wesley was here you wouldn't dare do such a thing."

"Just in fun indeed!" exclaimed Alice. "You'd better keep away from this pond in the future if you don't want to get into trouble." And both ducks, with wings spread and bills outstretched, came waddling towards him.

Weedly didn't wait any longer. He turned and ran.

He didn't run very far. After a minute he looked back, and the ducks were sitting on the bank again, practicing being sad, so he slowed down. He walked up along the brook, and then he took the path which went up into the woods. It was bright and sunny out in the meadow by the brook, and he could hear birds calling and dogs barking and a mowing machine whirring and the far-off whistle of a train, so that he knew that all around him the world was going on, full of happy, busy people. But in the woods it was dim and still. He walked along in a green twilight, and the sounds of the outside world were shut off from him by the tall silent tree trunks that, wherever he looked, seemed to close him in. There were sounds, but they were different—mysterious rustlings, and now and then the mournful whistle of a pewee, or the queer ringing notes of a wood thrush.

Lots of people like the mysteriousness of the woods, and so of course do lots of animals, even those that don't live there. Jinx loved the woods, and he used often to wander around in them by himself, and sometimes he would spend a whole day hiding in them, not to catch anything specially, but just for the fun of hiding. But Little Weedly was a pig, and pigs don't like to be alone much. So as he went along, he walked slower and slower. He didn't exactly jump when he heard little noises because he wasn't exactly scared, but he wasn't exactly comfortable about things either. It was fun pouncing out on people, but suppose something pounced out on him? He wondered what an owl was like. A big, fierce-looking bird, probably. Well, he'd said he was going to scare Old Whibley, and he was going to do it. But maybe he'd better not scare him too much.

So as he got nearer the big maple where Freddy had told him Old Whibley lived, he left the path and began creeping along through the underbrush. He crept from tree to tree like an Indian, and pretty soon he saw the maple. It was big and tall, and maybe fifty feet up, where it divided into great thick limbs, there was a hole. Weedly was peeking out from behind another trunk at it when a voice said sleepily: "Ho hum."

Weedly pulled his head back so quick that he bumped his nose on the tree trunk. When he had rubbed it till it stopped hurting he stuck it out again cautiously. A big bird was sitting on a branch a little above him. The bird had his eyes closed and seemed to be asleep, though he wasn't sleeping, like most birds, with his head underneath his wing. Weedly ducked back behind the tree again. "My goodness," he said to himself, "I wonder if that's Old Whibley. He doesn't look very ferocious. I wouldn't be afraid to scare him." And he was just getting ready to jump out and yell "Boo!" when the voice said: "Stop acting so silly and come out from behind that tree. I won't hurt you."

Weedly hesitated a minute and then he came out. "I—I thought you were asleep," he said. "I'm not afraid of you," he added quickly.

The bird opened one enormous yellow eye. "I'm not afraid of you either. That makes us even," he said. "Well, what do you want? Advice?"

"I—well, no, I guess not," said Weedly. "I was just wondering—are you Old Whibley?"

"That depends," said the bird, closing his eye again. "Who sent you?"

"Nobody, I just came. By myself."

"And you want to see Old Whibley?"

"Yes," said Weedly. "That is—no, not exactly."

The bird opened both big round eyes and stared at him. "Yes—no, yes—no. What kind of an answer is that? Either you do or you don't. Can't waste time with people that don't know their own minds. Old Whibley isn't home." He closed his eyes.

"Oh," said Weedly. He looked at the bird a minute and then he said: "Well, if you aren't Old Whibley, maybe you can tell me where I can find him?"

"You here again?" said the bird crossly, opening his left eye. "Well, tell me what you want with him. Then maybe I'll help you. Maybe I won't, too."

"I guess you don't know who I am," said Weedly, who was beginning to get cross. Silly old sleepyhead! Why couldn't he give a plain answer? "I'm Little Weedly, and Uncle Jinx—"

"I know," the bird interrupted. "He adopted you. Don't give me your family history."

"My family's all right," protested Weedly.

"I daresay," said the bird. "I don't want to hear about it, that's all."

"Oh, dear," said Weedly, "you get me all mixed up. It isn't anything important. I've just been having fun today scaring the animals on the farm, and Cousin Frederick said I couldn't scare Old Whibley, so I thought—"

"You thought you'd scare him," said the

. . . the birds suddenly swooped upon him.

bird. "Not a bad idea. You jump out and say 'Boo!' I suppose. Some people enjoy that kind of thing. But how are you going to work it? Old Whibley in the treetops, you on the ground. He wouldn't even hear you."

"Oh," said Weedly. "I didn't think of that."

"You wouldn't," said the other. "Still, if you could get up in his hole there, in that tree —eh? Then when he comes home, stick your nose out and say 'Boo!' "

"Oh, if I only could!" said Weedly. "But I can't climb a tree!"

"We can fix that," and the bird gave a hooting cry, and immediately another bird of the same kind, only a little smaller, came floating down from somewhere high up in the treetops and lit on the branch beside him. "My niece, Vera," he said to Weedly. "Vera, this is Weedly, who wants to scare Old Whibley. Wants us to take him up into Old Whibley's nest so he can jump out and say 'Boo!' at him when he comes home. Very funny idea."

"Very funny indeed," said Vera. But neither of the birds laughed.

"I guess," said Weedly doubtfully, "that I'd rather wait till some other day. I guess—" But he didn't finish, for the two birds suddenly swooped upon him, seized him with their strong beaks and claws, and with powerful flapping wings bore him up to the hole high in the trunk of the giant maple.

"There you are," said the first bird. "In you go. Hang on, there." And they tumbled him into the deep cavity, which was filled with sticks and leaves.

"Oh, dear!" said Weedly. "Oh, dear!" For his left ear and his tail had been badly pinched in the strong beaks, and the claws had dug into his plump little sides like big fishhooks. "How will I ever get down?" he moaned.

The two birds sat outside and looked at him. "Don't you worry," said Vera. "We'll carry you down after you've given Old Whibley a good scare." And she laughed for the first time.

"But when do you expect him?" said Weedly anxiously.

"Can't tell for sure," said the first bird. "But he ought to be back in a week or two."

And both birds opened their eyes very wide at him, and then burst into hoots of laughter and flew off.

"A week or two!" said Weedly. And then he thought of that hooting laughter. "I've heard that sound before," he said to himself. "And mother told me it was owls. Then if they're owls—why," he exclaimed, "I bet that was Old Whibley himself! Oh, dear!"

It wasn't very smart of Little Weedly not to have thought of that before. But of course he had never seen an owl. And then, although he thought it was funny to play tricks on other animals, it had never occurred to him that they might think it funny to play tricks on him. He wasn't very happy. Here he was in a hole in a tree fifty feet above the ground, and he didn't believe that those owls had any intention of coming back and taking him down. Not for a long time, anyway. He stuck his head out and yelled as loud as he could for his Uncle Jinx. But in the thick woods his voice didn't carry very far, and nobody heard him. And so, after he had yelled himself hoarse he did a very sensible thing. He curled up and went to sleep.

When he woke up it was beginning to get dark. At first he couldn't remember where he was. He got up sleepily and started to go out of the door, but just as he was going to step over the edge he looked down and saw the ground way below him, and he gave a yelp and jumped back. He stayed quiet after that, and it got darker and darker. He was hungry now, too. Back at the farm, he knew, the animals were all sitting down to their supper, talking and laughing and never giving a thought to the terrible danger he was in. He yelled for a while, but nobody came, so he went to sleep again.

The next time he woke up it was really dark. Out in the open fields, even when it is cloudy, it seldom gets as dark as it does in the deep woods. Weedly couldn't even see the door. At least he couldn't at first, but after a minute he knew where it was, because through it he saw a queer flickering light coming towards him through the trees. He didn't know what it was, but then at a little distance he saw another light, and another, and after a minute he heard voices.

"Help!" he yelled. "Uncle Jinx! Here I am. In Old Whibley's nest."

The lights came together and approached the tree, and he saw that it was Jinx and Freddy, and the two dogs, Robert and Georgie. And on each head was a little flickering green light.

"What on earth are you doing up there?" said Jinx. "We missed you at supper and we've been hunting all over the farm for you."

The light on Jinx's head seemed to fly apart into sparks, which floated up towards the owl's nest, and then came together again on the bark just over the door. Weedly saw now that they were fireflies.

"I want to get down," he said.

"Yeah," said Jinx drily, "I suppose you do. Well, you got up there somehow, so I suppose you can get down."

"But I can't," said Little Weedly. "That old owl carried me up here." And he told them how the trick he was going to play on

Old Whibley had been turned against himself. "He's a mean old thing," he said.

"That's where you're wrong," said Freddy. "There isn't a mean feather on Old Whibley's body. He did just right, if you ask me. You've been getting pretty fresh lately, Weedly."

"He's just played a joke on you," said Robert. "He wouldn't let you stay up there much longer. He'll be back before long to take you down. He's a good fellow."

There was a sudden loud hoot above them in the tree and Old Whibley's voice said: "Thanks for the compliments, gentlemen. You didn't know I was up here, so I take it they're sincere. Well, want me to bring him down?"

"I don't *want* him to bring me down," said Weedly. "He—he clawed me, carrying me up."

"Clawed, nothing," said Old Whibley contemptuously. "Want to know what it's like to be really clawed? I'll come in there and show you."

"You let me alone," said Weedly. "Uncle Jinx, you make him leave me alone."

"Suit yourself," said the owl. "Can't wait around here all night. Evening, gentlemen."

"He's gone," said Georgie. "He'll be back, all right. But look, Jinx, we can get Weedly down if we have some rope."

"I'd like to get him down," said Jinx. "Whibley's a good scout, but he don't know what a time I've had getting Weedly not to be so scared. If he's left up there all night, he may be just as scary as he was when he first came here, and then we'll have to train him all over again."

"If he was *my* nephew," began Freddy, but Jinx interrupted. "Well, he isn't," he said crossly.

"All right, all right," said the pig. "I have something to be thankful for, then. Well, come on, Georgie; you and I'll go get the rope." And they trotted off, the clusters of fireflies on their heads showing them the way like the little lanterns miners wear in their hats.

In half an hour they were back with the coil of rope. "We brought a ball of cord too," said Freddy, "because the rope will be too heavy to carry up all that distance."

"Hey, boys," Jinx shouted to the fireflies over Old Whibley's door, "go on up and find me the first branch directly over the door opening."

The fireflies broke apart and clustered again on a branch about three feet higher up.

"Fine!" said Jinx. "Hold it!" And he took one end of the cord in his mouth and began to climb. He went up past Weedly to the branch, dropped the end of the cord over it, and then sat on the branch and pulled the cord up and over it until the end reached the ground, where Freddy, who was awfully good at knots, tied it to the end of the rope. Then he and the dogs got hold of the other end of the cord and pulled on it until the rope was up over the branch.

Jinx took the rope end in his mouth and slithered down the trunk and into the nest, where he tied it around Weedly's waist.

"All ready, fellows?" he shouted. "Get a good grip on the rope now while I swing him out."

"We've got it," said Robert, as he and

Georgie and Freddy seized the rope in their teeth and braced themselves.

For a wonder, Weedly did not protest at being pushed out to dangle over fifty feet of thin air. Perhaps it was because he had so much confidence in his adopted uncle. He only gave one faint squeal as his feet slithered over the edge of the doorway. He kicked a little when Jinx shouted, "Lower away!" and he began descending in jerks. Some of the jerks were pretty jerky, too, particularly the one when Freddy fell over a log. But they brought him to ground safely. And then from up above them came Old Whibley's voice again.

"Nicely done, gentlemen."

"My gosh," said Jinx, "were you there all the time? You might have helped us."

"I might," said the owl.

"Letting us do all that work."

"I'm like you that way," said Old Whibley. "Never do work if I can get someone else to do it for me."

"Aw, rats!" said Jinx disgustedly. "I ought to know better than to argue with you." And he turned and cuffed Little Weedly severely. "Now," he said, "get along home. I'm not very pleased with this night's performance. You're not a very good sport, I guess. You can dish it out all right, but you can't take it."

"Don't be too hard on him, cat," said Old Whibley, and they all looked up in surprise. "It's easy enough—telling somebody else to be a good sport. Remember the time that rat down in Macy's barn—"

"All right, all right," Jinx interrupted hastily. "We haven't time for all this talk. It's Weedly's bedtime."

"Put him to bed then, and don't lecture," said the owl. "He hasn't done so badly, and if he's still mad at me, I guess I can bear it."

"I'm not mad at you, Mr.—Mr. Whibley," said Weedly.

"Good," said the owl. "Just remember, there's two ends to a joke. Depends on which end you get hold of whether it's fun or not. Now get along and take those lightning bugs out of here. They hurt my eyes."

Chapter 12

The next morning the three cows, Mrs. Wiggins and Mrs. Wurzburger and Mrs. Wogus, were in the upper pasture. They had had their breakfast and were lying under a tree by the stone wall, resting. Cows do a good deal of resting. They are not very ambitious, and few cows have ever made great names for themselves in the world. They would much rather sit around in the shade and talk. But they are often very wise animals, and their opinions are well worth listening to.

"It seems to me," said Mrs. Wurzburger, "that Freddy is making a mistake in being so friendly with these Snedekers. He's actually getting to like them. The first thing we know, he'll be saying that they ought to be allowed to take the silver teapot."

"I don't agree with you," said Mrs. Wogus. "He's a deep pig, that Freddy. He's got some scheme up his sleeve. He'll get rid of the Snedekers all right."

"Well," said Mrs. Wiggins, "I don't think I agree with either of you. I don't think Freddy has got any scheme up his sleeve. But on the other hand, I don't think he's making a mistake in being friendly with them. There are two things you can do if you have a disagreement with somebody. You can try to settle it by fighting, or you can try to settle it by being friendly with them. I don't think we'd get anywhere by fighting with the Snedekers. They'd just take the teapot and walk off, and we couldn't stop them. But if we make friends of them, they're as likely as not to decide the teapot isn't worth fighting about. As long as Aunt Effie feels we're her enemies, she's willing to fight with us. But if she feels we're her friends, she might come to value our friendship more than she does the teapot."

"Maybe you're right," said Mrs. Wurzburger. "I don't fancy Aunt Effie much myself. But I can see she has some good qualities. And it's funny, but you can like most anybody if you try hard enough."

"Except that horrible little pig that Jinx adopted," said Mrs. Wogus. "He jumped out at me yesterday when I was having lunch. I had a mouth full of clover, and I like to choked to death when he yelled. If I catch him around here again—"

"You're going to catch him in about two minutes," said Mrs. Wiggins. "Here he comes now, with Jinx."

"Well, my stars!" said Mrs. Wogus, getting up. "Can't we have any peace? I'll see you later, girls." And she started off across the pasture.

"Good land, we can't run away from a pig!" said Mrs. Wiggins. "Anyway, he won't try any funny business with Jinx around."

"Maybe you're right," said Mrs. Wogus,

and she came back and sat down again.

"Hello, girls," said Jinx breezily. He came up to them, but Weedly stopped and waited at a little distance.

"Good morning," said the cows. But none of them smiled.

"My goodness, why all the gloom?" said Jinx. "You all been eating poison ivy this morning or what?"

Mrs. Wogus looked at Mrs. Wurzburger and Mrs. Wurzburger looked at Mrs. Wiggins and Mrs. Wiggins said: "To tell you the truth, Jinx, we have been talking about Little Weedly. We don't think he's a very desirable person to have around this farm. We think you'd better send him back to his mother."

"Oh, go on!" said the cat. "Weedly's all right. He's just full of high spirits. You girls need shaking up a little. It'll do you good."

"It's our opinion that Weedly needs the shaking," put in Mrs. Wogus. "And believe me, he's going to get it if he cuts up any more of his didoes around the cowbarn."

"You'd better take him home before he gets hurt," said Mrs. Wurzburger.

"H'm, you mean it, don't you?" said Jinx, becoming serious. "Well, as a matter of fact, there's something in what you say. But Weedly and I had a little talk last night—after certain happenings up in the woods—and I don't think you'll have any more trouble with him."

"Where have I heard that before?" said Mrs. Wogus sarcastically.

"All right, all right," said Jinx. "But you can hear what he's got to say to you, anyway. Weedly, come here. What did you want to say to these ladies?"

"Well," said the pig, "I—I wanted to say that I'm sort of—I mean, I'm sorry I scared you. And I won't do it again."

"H'm," said Mrs. Wurzburger and Mrs. Wogus, and they looked at each other and shook their heads. But Mrs. Wiggins said: "Well, we can't ask any more in the way of an apology than that. We accept it."

"But you don't believe me, do you?" said Weedly. "And I do mean it, honestly I do."

"Yes, I guess you mean it now," said Mrs. Wogus. "But how about tomorrow, when you find me taking a nap in the cowbarn? I suppose you won't want to wake me up and scare me half to death, will you?"

"Well, I may want to," said Weedly. "But I won't do it. Because I—well, I didn't know what it was like to have mean jokes played on you. But now I know that there's two ends to a joke, and it depends on which end you get hold of whether it's fun or not."

"That sounds like Old Whibley," said Mrs. Wurzburger.

"It is Old Whibley," said Jinx. And he told them about what had happened in the woods.

"Well," said Mrs. Wurzburger, "I'm willing to give you another chance. Only let me warn you, Weedly—"

"Now, now," interrupted Mrs. Wiggins. "He's apologized, hasn't he? Well, let's just forget it. We'll just shake hands all round on it, and forget it." So Weedly shook hands with the three cows, and then he sat down and they talked about other things.

But they hadn't talked long when they saw Uncle Snedeker coming up the lane towards them. He had a stack of little white envelopes in his hand, and when he came up he handed each of them one, and then climbed the wall and went on up towards the woods.

"What on earth!" said Mrs. Wiggins. She had taken the envelope in her mouth, and now she got up and went over and dropped it on the top of the wall, and stood looking at it as if it might go off the next minute like a firecracker. "Now who would write me a letter?" she said.

"Why don't you open it and find out?" said Jinx, who had hooked a claw under the flap of his own envelope and was tearing it open.

"Well," said Mrs. Wiggins, "I don't know much about letters, and that's a fact. But I never saw one yet that wasn't better left unopened. The way I figure it, Jinx, is that what I don't know won't hurt me. As long as it isn't opened, I can think of lots of nice things it might be. But as soon as I open it, then it means I've got to do something. Even if it isn't anything but answering it."

Jinx had got the envelope open by this time, and he pulled out a card. "Well," he said, "if you know what this means, you're smarter than I am." And he said it as if there wasn't much doubt how smart he was.

The cows gathered around and looked at the card. On it was printed in very fancy letters: Mrs. Lucius Snedeker. And underneath was written: At home, Friday, August Seventh. Four o'clock. R.S.V.P.

"Why, that's today," said Mrs. Wogus.

"So it is," said Mrs. Wiggins. "So it is. Well, would you ever have thought that Mr. Snedeker's name was Lucius?"

"Yes," said Jinx, "but what does it mean?"

"Well, it's Aunt Effie's calling card," said Mrs. Wurzburger.

"Sure it is," said the cat. "But what's it say 'At home' for? We know she's at home. She don't have to send us notices about it. Of all the silly—"

"Wait a minute," interrupted Mrs. Wiggins. "Today's the day she gives us the tea-party. And it says here 'four o'clock.' Maybe it's kind of an invitation, and that's the time we're to come."

"Well, I still say it's silly," said Jinx. "If I was sending out invitations, I'd say, 'Please come to my teaparty at four o'clock.' And what's all this 'R.S.V.P.' stuff at the bottom?''

"I guess we'd better ask Freddy," said Mrs. Wiggins.

"Oh, Freddy!" exclaimed Jinx. "Freddy! What are you always asking Freddy about things for? He don't know any more than we do."

"Well, he certainly can't know any less," snapped Mrs. Wogus, and as the other cows agreed with her, they all went down to the pigpen.

Freddy came out to meet them. "Good morning," he said. "Well, I suppose you're getting your manners all polished up for the party this afternoon?"

"I guess my manners are good enough for any party this Aunt Effie can give," said Jinx.

"Sure they are," said Mrs. Wurzburger. "You've got nice manners, Jinx. The only trouble is," she added, as the cat's face broke into a pleased smile, "that you never use them."

"Oh, is that so!" said Jinx.

"I expect that's so of all of us," said Mrs.

"After you, my dear fellow."

Wiggins. "We know how to be polite all right, but we just don't take the trouble."

"Well, I don't see why you think we should waste all our politeness on these Snedekers," said the cat.

"I'll tell you why," said Freddy. "When Aunt Effie was talking to me she said she had never liked animals much, because she didn't think they had nice manners. I think we ought to show her that that isn't so. Because after all, it is Mrs. Bean that has taught us all the manners we know, and we'd want Mrs. Bean to be proud of us, wouldn't we?"

"Well, since you put it that way," said Jinx, "maybe you're right."

"So I've gone around to all the animals this morning," Freddy went on, "and asked them to practice up on their manners a little before going to the party. There! That's what I mean," he said, pointing to two chipmunks who were standing before a crevice in the stone wall, bowing to each other.

"No, no, Roger," said the first chipmunk. "After you, my dear fellow." And he put one paw over his heart and bowed deeply.

But the other chipmunk also bowed. "I wouldn't dream of preceding you, my honored friend," he said. "After you, Horace, I beg." And they kept on bowing and making polite speeches, while the other animals watched them, until at last as they both made one specially deep bow at the same moment, their heads came together with a crack, and at once they dove together for the hole, out of which came angry squeaks and a sound of scrabbling. And in a minute out popped Roger. He ran over to Freddy.

"He bit me!" he said angrily. "That's what I get for trying to be polite to him. You just wait till I catch him in the open, the big bully. I'll show him!"

"Well, I don't know," said the pig. "You can't expect him to be polite all at once, you know. It's hard to learn to be really polite. I'd try again, if I were you. After all, it was an accident when you banged your heads. It wasn't anything to fight about."

"Would you?" said the chipmunk. "Well, all right if you say so." And he ran off.

"My, my!" said Jinx. "Aren't we noble!

It's easy to see it wasn't your head that got bumped, Freddy."

"Keep still, Jinx," said Mrs. Wiggins. "See here, Freddy; did you get some sort of a card from Aunt Effie?"

"Yes, an invitation to the teaparty."

"That's what we thought it was," said the cow. "But it had some letters on it, and we didn't know what they meant. We came down to ask you."

"You mean R.S.V.P.?" asked Freddy, who knew perfectly well that she did, for he too had been wondering what they meant, and had nearly torn his dictionary apart trying to find them.

"Of course we do," said Jinx. "Quit stalling, Freddy. What do they mean?"

"Why, they're—goodness, everybody knows that! They're an—an abbreviation."

"Yeah? And what's that?"

"Well, if instead of writing my name all out —F-r-e-d-d-y, like that, I just wrote an F, that would be an abbreviation."

"You mean the letters stand for four words, is that it?" said the cat. "Well, don't take all day. What are the words?"

Freddy laughed easily. "My goodness," he said, "don't you know? Why, I thought anybody knew that! Dear, dear, to think you don't know a simple little thing like that!"

"Come *on*, Freddy," said Mrs. Wurzburger. "Do you know?"

"Certainly I do."

"Well, then, tell us."

"Why it—it means . . ." Freddy broke off. "Have you got your card with you? Yours might be different, you know. I wouldn't want to tell you wrong."

"Here," said Mrs. Wogus, and put her card down in front of him.

"H'm," said Freddy. "R.S.V.P. Yes, it's the same. Why it's—let me see. R. That's—er—that's—why, it's refreshments. Yes, that's what it means. See? It's as simple as that."

"It's like pulling teeth to get this out of you," said Mrs. Wiggins, "but we're going to have the rest of it. There are three more letters, Freddy."

"So there are," said the pig, looking surprised. "Well, well. Refreshments served—

yes, served—very—let me see. Oh, yes. Re-freshments served very promptly," he brought out triumphantly. "That's what it means. Goodness, to think you didn't know that!"

"So that's it?" said Mrs. Wiggins. "Now that's the kind of invitation I like to get. Well, come along, girls. We might as well go back to the pasture and practice a little politeness ourselves. Because the politer you are at a party, the more you can eat without anybody noticing it."

Chapter 13

All the animals on the farm, and even some who lived up in the woods, had been invited to the party. The Snedekers had been up at dawn, baking pies and cakes and cookies, and cutting sandwiches, and by half-past three everything was ready. Aunt Effie, in her best black silk dress and a new bonnet, was presiding over the teatable in the parlor, and Uncle Snedeker, in a new blue suit much too tight for him, was hurrying about, putting the finishing touches to everything, arranging

207

chairs for the larger animals and footstools
and garden benches for the smaller ones, so
that there would be no crowding and confusion.

Outside in the barnyard the animals had
gathered, and they stood around in little
groups, practicing their company manners
until it was time to go in. At last Freddy, who
had been watching the clock through the kitchen window, turned around and waved his
forelegs for attention.

"All right, animals," he shouted. "It's five
minutes of four. Time to go in. No crowding, please. And when you get inside remember, this is a party, not a football game. And
for goodness' sake, don't *grab!*" Then he
turned to Hank. "I hope everything'll go all
right," he said. "Some of these animals have
never been in the house before, and you know
how curious squirrels are. I hope they won't
get snooping around upstairs."

"Don't know as I've been in there more
than once myself," said the horse. "Mrs. Bean
took me in to see the new wallpaper, last time
the parlor was papered. Right pretty 'twas,

too. But I dunno; I guess I won't go in today. I feel kind of out of place in a parlor, Freddy, and that's the truth."

"Nonsense!" said the pig. "You'd be an ornament to any parlor, Hank. You're too modest."

" 'Tain't modesty," said the horse. "It's my shoes. 'Tain't right for me to go clumping around on Mrs. Bean's nice carpets with these things on. And it'll be pretty crowded in there, and if I was to step on somebody's toe—"

"They'd let you know all right," said Freddy. "Well, you must suit yourself. I must be getting in." And he joined the line that was filing in the front door, like the animals into the ark.

Uncle Snedeker greeted the animals at the door, and they went on into the parlor to pay their respects to Aunt Effie. When they had shaken hands with her, they found places on chairs and benches along the wall, where they talked in low voices about the weather and such other topics as they thought suited to tea-parties, and tried not to look too greedily at

the platters piled up with cakes and sandwiches. It was probably one of the politest
teaparties ever held in New York State.

Freddy went up to the teatable and bowed
low over Aunt Effie's hand. "Good afternoon,
madam," he said. "I trust I find you in good
health?"

"Excellent," said Aunt Effie. "So nice of
you to come."

Freddy sat down on the pink ottoman. In
a rocking chair next to him was Mrs. Wiggins.

"A lovely day for a party," said Freddy.

The cow put up one hoof and spoke behind
it. "There's Webb up there on the picture
frame," she whispered. "Do you suppose he
got an invitation too?"

From where Freddy sat he could see out
into the front hall. Charles, followed by his
wife, Henrietta, and their twenty-seven children, had just filed through the front door.
"Charles is coming late so he can have an audience for his grand entrance," said the pig.
"Oh, look!"

Charles had evidently planned to lead his
family into the parlor, but just as he started

through the door with his most pompous strut, Henrietta rushed up and with several sharp pecks on the ear, drove him back. "Ladies first, you dope!" she said crossly, in a voice that everybody in the parlor could hear. There was a subdued clucking and cackling for a moment, and then at the head of her family the hen marched in and up to the table, where she held out a claw to Aunt Effie. "Good afternoon," she said. "May I present my daughters? This is Dinah, and this is Cackletta, and this is Calpurnia . . ." She went through the whole list, and Aunt Effie shook hands with each. At the end Henrietta paused, then said with a sniff: "And this is my husband."

But Charles, though he had brought up the tail of the procession, was not going to be robbed of his chance to make a speech. "I cannot tell you, madam," he said, "what a pleasure it is to me to be present on this auspicious occasion. An occasion, I may say, which is without parallel in the annals of Bean. Yes, I believe I can truthfully say, without fear of contradiction—"

But he got no further, for at that moment Hank, who had finally decided to come in, entered the room. He was rather nervous and held his head high as he clumped up to the table, and so did not see Charles, who gave one frightened squawk as a big hoof thumped down within an inch of his tailfeathers, and fluttered up to a perch on the sofa.

"Why, this is very nice," said Aunt Effie. "I'm glad you came, Hank."

"Well, so'm I, ma'am," said the horse. "At least, I guess I am. I better not shake hands with you, I guess. If it ain't polite to shake hands with gloves on, as I've heard Mrs. Bean say, why it certainly ain't, to shake 'em with shoes on. I'll just move over here in the corner out of the way."

"It's funny how something always seems to interrupt Charles's speeches," said Mrs. Wiggins to Freddy.

"It isn't so queer," said the pig, "when you remember that he's practically always making a speech, and so everything that happens is bound to be an interruption."

"That's so," said Mrs. Wiggins with a

laugh, and then she said: "My land, I mustn't get to laughing, or I'll shake this chair to pieces. Don't you say anything funny, Freddy."

Uncle Snedeker had come in and was passing around the refreshments.

"Sakes alive, Freddy," whispered Mrs. Wiggins, "I can't manage a teacup. What'll I do?"

"Ask Uncle Snedeker to put it on the table beside you. Then you can sip a little every now and then. Nobody ever comes to a tea-party to drink tea, anyway. Golly, look at Charles. He's trying to show off. I hope he doesn't drop it."

The rooster had picked up his teacup in one claw. He dipped his beak into it with a very refined air, and then turned to Aunt Effie. "Delicious, madam, delicious," he said. "Where do you get your tea, may I ask?" But before she could answer, the handle slipped in his claw, the cup turned upside down, and the tea splashed down onto the sofa.

"Eh, she gets it all over the sofa, evidently," said Uncle Snedeker, rushing up with a napkin. "Clumsy critter! Eh, that's what comes of asking poultry to a party. If I had my way—"

"That'll do, Snedeker," said Aunt Effie. "He didn't do it on purpose. Leave him alone. There, there," she said to Charles, who, to hide his confusion, was trying to crawl under the sofa, "come out, Charles, and let me pour you another cup. Accidents will happen. You mustn't let it spoil the party for you."

"You—you're very kind, ma'am," said the crestfallen rooster. He climbed back on the sofa, keeping his head turned away from Henrietta, who was glaring angrily at him. "No more tea, thank you," he said. "If I might just have one of these little cakes—"

Some of the animals had shown an inclination to giggle, and Little Weedly, who was sharing a saucer of milk with Jinx, choked and had to be whacked on the back, and finally led outside. But most of them were much impressed with Aunt Effie's good nature.

"My goodness, she certainly was nice about it," said Mrs. Wiggins to Freddy. "Maybe you're right about her, after all."

"Well, she's the hostess," said the pig, "and she's not going to let anything spoil the party. There's something to be said for politeness, all right. You know, I never exactly thought about it before, but Mrs. Bean's pretty polite. She'd do anything rather than hurt anybody's feelings."

" 'Tisn't the same kind of politeness," said Mrs. Wiggins. "Mrs. Bean's polite all the time. But Aunt Effie's only polite when her etiquette book says she ought to be, and that's when she's having a party, or maybe when somebody else is being polite to her. I guess with her it's just manners, and not real politeness."

"Maybe," said Freddy. "But just the same, it gives me an idea." He was thoughtful for a minute.

"What is it?" asked the cow.

Freddy shook his head. "Maybe it wouldn't work, at that. Just the same," he said, "I'm going to try to keep the Snedekers here until the Beans come home. Why, they'll be back in about three weeks more." He got up and walked over to the teatable.

Aunt Effie, who had been chatting with the two ducks, turned to him. "May I offer you a cookie?" she said. "Alice and Emma," she went on, "have been telling me that you're going to give a play."

Freddy sat down and told her about it. They were going to have it, he said, in about two weeks. Aunt Effie was interested and was asking some questions when Peter, the bear, came up to say he must be getting home. "It's a very nice party you've given us, ma'am," he said, "and I'm sure we're all very grateful."

"That's very kind of you," said Aunt Effie. "But won't you stay a while longer? And did Snedeker give you that jar of honey? I got it specially for you at the store today."

"I'm sorry," said Peter, "but I really must be getting along. Perhaps I can have the honey some other time."

"You must take it with you, then," said Aunt Effie, and she had Uncle Snedeker get the honey and put it in a paper bag, so Peter could carry it.

Most of the animals thought this was pretty nice, but Henrietta, who had been talking to

Jinx, gave a sarcastic cluck and said to the cat: "Trying to get on the right side of us! Well, she needn't think she can get the teapot that way."

But Aunt Effie had overheard the remark. She straightened up very stiff and stared angrily at the hen for a minute, then her expression softened, and she said: "I'm sorry you feel that way about my party, Henrietta. I would like to say to you, and to all the animals, that I gave you the party because I like to give parties, and not to get on the right side of anybody. Freddy understands this, I am sure," and she looked at the pig, who nodded agreement. "There are certain differences of opinion between us," she went on, "but I see no reason why these should be brought up in a purely social gathering."

The other animals looked reprovingly at Henrietta, and even Jinx muttered: "Pipe down, can't you? Don't spoil the party."

But Henrietta was not easy to stop. "I'm sorry you heard my remark," she said, "but since the subject has been brought up—"

"Just a minute," interrupted Mrs. Wiggins

in her deep booming voice, and Henrietta, who respected Mrs. Wiggins more than any other animal on the farm, stopped. "We all know how you feel, Henrietta," she went on, "and we agree with you. But my land, there's a time and place for everything. Aunt Effie, in giving this party, and we, in coming to it, agreed to forget about our differences for the afternoon. If you can't do that, what did you come for?"

Henrietta all at once looked pretty ashamed of herself. Few people have seen a hen look ashamed, and certainly none of the Bean animals had ever seen Henrietta look that way. But then they had never heard Mrs. Wiggins rebuke anyone so strongly before, for she was one of the mildest cows that ever lived, and cows as a class are extremely mild.

There was silence for a minute while Henrietta tried to think of something to say, and then to everyone's surprise Charles hopped down from the sofa and walked boldly over to her side. "There may be a time and a place for everything," he said angrily to Mrs. Wiggins, "but I feel that you have selected them

" . . . there's a time and a place for everything."

very poorly for doing a gross injustice to my wife. A gross injustice and a public injustice. Yes, I repeat. My poor little wife—"

"Oh, shut up!" snapped Henrietta, turning on him suddenly in a fury. "Your poor little wife indeed! I never heard such nonsense. And don't you dare to criticize Mrs. Wiggins. She is perfectly right!"

"Well, but—but—" stammered the bewildered Charles. The animals were beginning to snicker, and the snicker grew to a giggle, and the giggle to a roar of laughter, in which after staring at each other for a moment both Charles and Henrietta joined.

The hen walked slowly over to the teatable. "I wish to apologize—" she began.

"No, no," said Aunt Effie, who was laughing herself. "No apologies. It's all forgotten. Here, I think you haven't tried one of my seed cakes. —And now, animals," she continued as the laughter subsided, "I want to say this to you. I only hope that you are enjoying this party half as much as I am."

Jinx jumped on a chair. "Three cheers for Aunt—" he began, but got no further, for

Robert pulled him down.

"You can't cheer at a teaparty!" said the dog. "Didn't Freddy tell us to remember this isn't a football game?"

"Eh?" said Jinx. "Oh, I get you. Fellow animals," he said, "let's give Aunt Effie a great big hand." And he clapped his paws together, and all the other animals did the same. I don't suppose anybody had ever seen Aunt Effie look so happy before. She was so happy that when she took a sip of tea she forgot to stick her little finger out. And over in the doorway, where he was bringing in two big cakes, Uncle Snedeker said: "Well, perfume my handkerchief! Eh, Effie, you don't look a day over sixteen!" Which of course wasn't strictly true, but it pleased Aunt Effie some more.

So the party got going again after that, and they ate up the two cakes and all the sandwiches and cookies and pie, and told stories and jokes, all in the politest way imaginable, and then they shook hands with Aunt Effie and Uncle Snedeker and said what a good time they had had, and went home.

Chapter 14

After the party the silver teapot remained in full view on the teatable in the parlor. But there was no way for the animals to get it. The parlor door was locked, and Aunt Effie had the key. Every day she went in twice; once in the morning to dust and see that everything was all right, and once in the afternoon to have tea. Sometimes she invited Uncle Snedeker to tea, and sometimes one of the animals. The animals really enjoyed it. As Robert said: "It isn't as much trouble as I would have supposed, being polite for half an hour. It's sort of like a game, really. And there's always something good to eat."

Aunt Effie enjoyed it, too. "I wish our friends out in Orenville could see what nice manners these animals have," she said to Uncle Snedeker. "They'd be put to shame, that's what they would. Why that Freddy is downright courtly."

But the animals did not relax their watch on the teapot. Day and night, the Webbs stood guard on the frame of Washington Crossing the Delaware, and under the parlor floor one or another of the mice was always ready to gallop out and give the alarm if the Snedekers started to go. The mice, indeed, had made one gallant attempt to rescue the teapot. Late one night, after the Snedekers were in bed, they had started to gnaw a hole in the floor under the sofa. It was good stiff gnawing, for the Bean house was well built, but they had figured that by early morning they could have a hole large enough to slide the teapot through. But four mice gnawing make a good deal of noise in the middle of the night. Aunt Effie heard them. She came downstairs, found the hole, which was about as big as a dime, put a scuttle of coal over it, and in the morning Uncle Snedeker patched it with a piece of tin.

In the meantime, the animals kept the Snedekers pretty busy around the farm. They called Aunt Effie's attention to things that had to be done; and Aunt Effie sent Uncle Snedeker out to do them. Even Mrs. Webb thought of something to keep them busy. She persuaded a family of small moths to come in and fly around in Aunt Effie's bedroom. Aunt Effie spent three days taking all the clothing and blankets outdoors and sweeping and beating and shaking them.

Freddy had worked day and night on his play. By August 17th, ten days after the party, it was done, and the parts were given out to the different animals. Aunt Effie had told him that she would like very much to see it, but that she couldn't promise to stay later than the 20th.

"We'll try to give it before that," said Freddy, "but I wish we had a little more time.

If we only had until the 25th—"

Aunt Effie looked at him sharply. "You're expecting the Beans on the 25th, aren't you?" she asked.

"Well, yes," said Freddy, looking embarrassed.

"You know very well we're not going to wait for the Beans," said Aunt Effie. "I dislike to mention it, because you animals have been very pleasant, but you must understand that I haven't changed my mind about the teapot. I'm going to take it with me."

"Oh, no, you're not," Freddy said, but he said it to himself. Aloud he said: "Well, I'll have to hurry our rehearsals along, then. And if you'll stay, we'll give it on the evening of the 20th." So Aunt Effie said she would.

If you had visited the Bean farm during the next three days, you wouldn't have supposed that there was an animal on the place. But if you had walked around, through the barns, and past the pigpen, and up along the stone wall, you would every now and then have heard a mumbling sound. And if you had hunted to see where it came from, you would have found some animal securely tucked away in a quiet place, repeating his part under his breath. None of the parts were very long. The whole play was pretty short, for Freddy had very sensibly decided that a short play where everybody knows his part is much better than a long one, where the actors keep forgetting and having to start over again.

It was a very distinguished audience that faced the curtain, made out of two old horse blankets, in the big barn the evening of August 20th. In the front row, on chairs brought from the house, sat the Snedekers, and besides them the sheriff, and Mr. Weezer, President of the Centerboro Bank, who was an old friend of Freddy's. And behind and around them was a dense crowd of animals—cows and dogs and pigs and sheep and horses from neighboring farms, and wild animals from woods and fields,—raccoons and porcupines and rabbits and squirrels and woodchucks and even a few deer. Sniffy Wilson, the skunk, with his father and mother and three little sisters, was there, and every beam and rafter was crowded with birds. Even Old

Whibley and his niece, Vera, were among those present.

Promptly at eight o'clock, Freddy stepped out between the horse blankets. "Ladies and gentlemen," he said, "owing to the amount of work which it has taken to produce this play, it has been impossible to print programs. I will therefore announce that the scene of the play is the court of Queen Elizabeth. The time is somewhere between 1620 and 1940. The part of Queen Elizabeth will be taken by Mrs. Wiggins. The other actors will announce their own characters as they enter. Lights!"

Immediately the electric light which hung over the heads of the audience went out, and two lights behind the curtain were switched on. Freddy disappeared, and Robert and Georgie came out and seizing the lower corners of the blankets in their teeth, pulled them down and dragged them to one side, disclosing Queen Elizabeth, seated on her throne, attended by two ladies-in-waiting, and surrounded by her courtiers.

Mrs. Wiggins looked truly regal. Her

throne was the back seat of the old phaeton which the animals had brought back with them from their famous trip to Florida. Around her neck was a wide paper ruff; she wore an ermine robe made out of an old sheet, and a small crown of gilt paper perched between her horns. Alice and Emma, the two ladies-in-waiting, sat on the front seat chatting gaily, but pausing occasionally to wipe away a tear. And around the phaeton crowded the other animals, dressed as courtiers in odds and ends of old clothing which Mr. and Mrs. Bean had discarded and which Freddy had saved to disguise himself with in his detective work.

After a minute Little Weedly stepped forward. He had a gingham apron tied over his shoulders like a cloak and on his head was an old hat of Mrs. Bean's with a long feather in it. He looked quite dashing.

WEEDLY

Sir Walter Raleigh is my name
And I have come my bride to claim:
The fair and beauteous Lady Alice,
Who works here in your Majesty's palace.

THE QUEEN

O have you, sir, indeed? And may
I ask just how you get that way?
If you were secretly engaged—

WEEDLY

We were, ma'am, please don't be enraged.

THE QUEEN

Then you must take the consequences
Of this most serious of offenses:
A secret with the Queen unshared.
I wonder, sir, that you have dared
To come with such a bold request.
—Unless perhaps you speak in jest?

WEEDLY (*firmly*)

The Lady Alice I shall wed.

THE QUEEN (*angrily*)

Guards, take him out! Chop off his head!

Four rabbits wearing paper hats and carrying
swords made out of laths marched in and surrounded Weedly. But Alice fluttered down

from the front seat of the phaeton and threw
herself at the Queen's feet.

ALICE

O pause, Your Majesty, I pray
 Before you have him led away
 And do not judge him too severely
 Because, you see, I love him dearly.
 And if you must chop someone's head,
 Don't chop off his: chop mine instead.

THE QUEEN

I'm not particularly keen
 On chopping anybody's bean.
 What makes me mad is never knowing,
 In my own palace, how things are going,
 Who's coming in, who's going out,
 What's going on. I'm told about
 Nothing at all. I think it's mean.
 Nobody ever tells the Queen.

And then Mrs. Wiggins sang the following
song:

>   Nobody ever tells me;
>   Nobody lets me know.

"*Guards, take him out!*"

Wars are fought and groceries bought
    And people come and go,
But what is the use of being a Queen
    To sit in a marble hall
If nobody tells you anything, anything,
    Any-thing at all?

I want to know all the gossip
    That all the courtiers know,
Who had a fight and stayed out all night
    And who has a brand new beau.
But you sit on a throne and you're all
  alone
    And if anyone comes to call
They simply won't tell you anything, any-
  thing,
    Any-thing at all.

There was a good deal of applause, both
from actors and audience, but the Queen held
up her hoof and said:

Thank you, my friends, you're very kind,
But it hasn't made me change my mind.

Well, then there was an argument between
the Queen and Alice and Little Weedly,
which I won't repeat from the play because it

was pretty long, and not really in Freddy's best style. He had had to write the play pretty fast in order to get it produced before the 20th, and so he hadn't done it very carefully, and some of it, as perhaps you have noticed, was pretty slangy. Hardly the kind of talk a queen would have used. But all the actors took their parts so well that the audience didn't notice it.

Well, by telling the Queen little bits of gossip that she hadn't yet heard, they got her into a better humor, and she agreed not to chop off Sir Walter's head just yet. Of course Sir Walter was pleased at this and he thanked her so nicely that she said:

Sir Walter, your politeness and your high-
  flown elocution,
Though not half so entertaining as a
  public execution,
Do at least deserve some sort of a reward.
  What shall I grant you?

SIR WALTER

Your Majesty can let me marry Lady Alice, can't you?

The Queen began to look rather cross again, but Sir Walter said quickly:

> O Your Majesty, pray don't be angry. I
>   am just suggesting
> That the court would find a wedding
>   just about as interesting
> As an execution.

THE QUEEN

> Why, that's true, Sir Walter.
>   A beheading
> Isn't half as entertaining as a really bang-
>   up wedding.
> Very well then. It is settled. Get out the
>   invitations.
> Let all the guests provide themselves
>   with suitable donations.
> For the wedding shall take place tomor-
>   row afternoon at three.
> I suppose I'll have to give you something,
>   too. Now let me see.
> Get out the royal jewels. We will make a
>   quick selection.
> Something neat, I think, in rubies, to
>   match the bride's complexion.

So Emma went to the harness closet in the corner and dragged out an old tin teapot full of bits of broken glass that the animals had collected. She brought it over and was just going to dump it out in front of the Queen when Jinx, as a G-man, in an old felt hat and carrying a cap pistol came in, pretending to push Hank in front of him. Hank was dressed as a pirate. He had borrowed Uncle Snedeker's big hat and with Henrietta's help had built it up with a lot of old ostrich feathers until it was nearly two feet high. Around his waist was a belt through which was thrust a cardboard cutlass.

"Your Majesty," said Jinx, "I picked up this guy out back of the palace. He was acting kind of suspicious so I brought him in." Jinx had refused to speak his lines in verse because he said it was sissy. He and Freddy had had quite an argument about it, but as you probably know, when a cat makes up his mind you might as well let him do what he wants to, for he'll do it anyway.

So then the Queen asked Hank what he was doing out back of the palace.

HANK

Your Majesty, it's a long long story,
Full of shooting, and very gory.
For since I was but a little lad
I've been a pirate, bold and bad.
I've sunk tall ships and taken their
    treasure
And I've spent it all on fun and pleasure.
And when I heard of the wealth untold
That Your Majesty has in gems and gold
I thought I'd find where you conceal it
And then sneak in at night and steal it.
My name is Captain William Kidd,
But for what I've done and for what I've
    did
I won't repent nor ask for quarter
Although I've done what I hadn't orter.

THE QUEEN

Why goodness me, you're a very bad man!

CAPTAIN KIDD

I am, your Majesty, I am.

THE QUEEN

And you've just made, too, a very bad
   rhyme.

CAPTAIN KIDD

Give me time, Your Majesty, give me
   time.
As a man I'm bad, and you and I know it,
But just the same I'm a pretty good poet,
And so, before you have me led off
To put me in jail, or chop my head off
All in accord with your royal will,
Give me a chance to prove my skill.

THE QUEEN

Very well, very well, we'll give you a trial,
But the first rhyme you miss, I warn you,
   I'll
Send you out to be executed.

CAPTAIN KIDD

Your Majesty's judgment can't be dis-
   puted.

THE QUEEN

Very well, then. Find me a rhyme for
   "dutiful."

CAPTAIN KIDD

Your Majesty is extremely beautiful.

THE QUEEN

Very neat, Captain. How about "twenty"?

CAPTAIN KIDD

The Captain liked gold, and wherever he
    went he
Always found plenty.

THE QUEEN

Thirty.

CAPTAIN KIDD

Dirty.

THE QUEEN

Forty.

CAPTAIN KIDD

Warty.

THE QUEEN

Fifty.

CAPTAIN KIDD

Shifty.

THE QUEEN

Well that's pretty good. But how about "sixty"?

CAPTAIN KIDD

When she's offered tea or coffee, the Queen always picks tea.

THE QUEEN

Let's try a long word, like "circumlocutional."

CAPTAIN KIDD

It's unconstitutional.

THE QUEEN

Well, you've saved your head, I guess, this time,
For you don't make sense, but you do make rhyme,
And that's all that anyone asks of a poet.
But tell me a word, in case you know it,
That hasn't any rhyme.

CAPTAIN KIDD

> Well, let me see:
> Your stopping at sixty was a good thing for me.
> Can your Majesty find a rhyme for "seventy"?

THE QUEEN

> Why of course. I—I—

Well the Queen stammered and broke down and couldn't go on, because of course she couldn't find any rhyme. Somebody suggested "eleventy," but she shook her head and said no, that wasn't fair. And then she laughed, and said she guessed she'd have to appoint the Captain to the post of court poet. Only he'd have to promise not to steal the royal jewels.

After that there was a lot of yelling outside and Charles came in as an Indian chief, at the head of a band of Indians who were mostly his daughters, with a few other birds who had wanted to take part in the play. They all had extra feathers stuck into their own feathers around their heads, and Charles had on a piece of old red flannel petticoat for a blanket, and they did a war dance for the Queen. Uncle Snedeker was rather nervous during this performance, even though he knew that of course these Indians were nothing but chickens. The dance was very exciting with lots of yelling in it, and when it was over Charles made a rather too long speech which nobody understood very well, and then the Queen invited them to stay for the wedding. And she was just going to select a present for Alice from among the royal jewels when Emma stepped up and announced to the Queen that it was time for her to take her royal nap.

So the Queen had Emma take the jewels back to the harness closet, and then she took off her crown and put her head down against the back seat. Then all the courtiers lay down where they were, because of course at court everybody has to do what the Queen does. And the lights were turned out.

Chapter 15

Some of the animals thought the play was over, and started to go, but Freddy came out and asked them to remain seated. "And I hope you will please refrain from talking," he said, "as this is a very important scene in the play."

There was some whispering on the stage, and several people seemed to be moving around, and then the lights were turned on. There was a hitch in starting the play going again because Mrs. Wiggins really had gone to sleep and it took some time to wake her up, and after that it was several minutes before she remembered where she was. Then when she did, she got to laughing, and everybody had to wait for that. But pretty soon she quieted down and put her crown on again, and sent Emma for the royal jewels. But the jewels and the royal teapot were gone. Somebody had stolen them.

Well, the Queen was pretty upset. But although the teapot wasn't of much value, she seemed more worried about it than about the jewels, because she was accustomed to having tea out of it every afternoon. Her tea wouldn't seem the same out of any other teapot, she said. Then Sherlock Holmes was sent for, and he came in—it was Freddy, of course, in false whiskers and a peaked cap—and while the G-man lined up Captain Kidd and the Indians against the wall and asked them questions, Sherlock Holmes went around examining things through a magnifying glass, and trying to detect something.

Pretty soon the Queen decided that she

wanted to get down from her throne and look in the closet herself to make sure that the things really weren't there. She started to get out of the phaeton, and Sir Walter took off his cloak and threw it down on the floor so she could step on it. It was a very courtly act, but unfortunately as he took off the cloak something flew out of it and tinkled on the floor. It was one of the pieces of glass.

"My diamond sceptre!" exclaimed the Queen. "Guards, seize him!"

This part of the play was mostly in prose, as Freddy hadn't had time to turn it all into verse.

So the rabbits came in, and in spite of Sir Walter's protests, and Alice's tears, they marched him away to have his head chopped off.

The G-man was being a G-man for all he was worth, and hustling the Indians around and he grabbed the Indian chief and shook him.

"Hey, take it easy, Jinx," protested the chief. "All this rough stuff isn't in the play."

But Jinx went right on playing his part.

Sherlock Holmes went round examining . . .

"Quiet, you!" he said and gave the chief an extra shake, and another of the royal jewels flew out of his blanket.

"Guards!" shouted the Queen, and then the rabbits came in and led the chief away.

"Hey, your Majesty," said the G-man, "I think I'd better search all these guys."

So he did. He searched Captain Kidd, and didn't find anything, but then he began searching the others, and on each one he found one of the jewels. And each time he found one, the guards came in and led away the culprit to have his head chopped off.

"Why, this is terrible," said the Queen. "It's a conspiracy."

"It's very queer," said Sherlock Holmes. "They can't all be guilty."

"They've all got stolen goods on 'em," said the G-man.

"How about you?" said Sherlock Holmes.

"Why I—I didn't take anything," said the G-man.

"Search him, guards," said the Queen.

So they searched the G-man, and sure enough, he had a stolen jewel in his hatband,

and then he was led off.

Now there were only Alice and Emma and Sherlock Holmes and Captain Kidd and the Queen left.

"Well, Captain," said the Queen, "you at least are innocent. And Sherlock Holmes wasn't here when the robbery took place, so he is innocent. But the Lady Alice and the Lady Emma—"

"Your Majesty," said Lady Emma, trembling, "I just found one of the royal jewels in my pocket. But I don't know how it got there."

"Oh, your Majesty," sobbed Alice, "so did I."

"So!" said the Queen, frowning terribly. "You don't know how it got there, eh? Guards!" And the two ducks were led away, weeping bitterly.

"I can't help feeling, your Majesty," said Sherlock Holmes, "that you are perhaps making a mistake."

"A mistake?" said the Queen. "The Queen never makes mistakes!"

"I beg Your Majesty's pardon," said Sherlock Holmes. "You have sent practically the entire court out to have their heads chopped off. You have recovered most of the crown jewels. But where is the royal teapot? It must be here in the throne room, because no one has left, except to be executed."

"You have searched the room?" said the Queen.

"I have. And it is not to be found. But I still say, it must be in this room."

"Well, I haven't got it," said the Queen crossly. "It's too large to be concealed in a pocket." She began patting herself all over, as if expecting to find the teapot on her person, then suddenly she gave them a horrified look. "Goodness gracious!" she said. "I've got one of the jewels myself!" Then she drew herself up, and it was a fine piece of acting. She looked every inch a queen. "Justice must be done," she said regally. "Guards, take me out and chop off my head."

"Oh, your Majesty, please!" protested Sherlock Holmes. "Even though you did have one of the jewels concealed on your person, it belongs to *you*. You can't steal from yourself. And so it would not be right to execute yourself."

"H'm," said the Queen, "perhaps you're right."

"And besides," continued Sherlock Holmes, "I know now who the thief is. I know who he must be. For there is only one thing in this room that I haven't looked into, which is still large enough to conceal the teapot. And that is Captain Kidd's hat." And he rushed at the Captain and tore off his hat, and the teapot rolled out on the floor.

"Guards, do your duty," said the Queen, and then as the rabbits surrounded Hank, she said: "Wait a minute. Before you have your head chopped off, Captain, perhaps you'd care to explain."

So the Captain did. It was the teapot he had come to steal, he said. He didn't want the jewels, because his piracy had been so successful that he had plenty. But he wanted the teapot for his old mother, who had never had a really nice one. Being a pirate, he was away from home a good deal, and his mother was pretty lonely. Of course, she didn't know that he was a pirate; she thought he was in the real estate business. And she had said that if she only had a nice teapot, to have tea out of in the long evenings, she would be much happier. The Captain painted such an affecting picture of his poor old mother, sitting by the window, waiting for her son to come home, and wishing for a teapot, that the Queen was quite touched.

"It is too bad," she said, "that you didn't tell me all this. I would have been glad to send the old lady a nice teapot. Now, of course, you will have to lose your head. But I promise you that I'll send her the teapot anyway."

The Captain said that made him feel much better. "And I should tell you, your Majesty," he said, "that I didn't want all these other courtiers to lose their heads. While you were taking your nap I stole the jewels, and hid the teapot in my hat, and then I sneaked around and hid one jewel in the clothes of each person in the room. I thought since there were so many of them, you would just have them put into prison, and then when all the jewels turned up you would be so happy that you would forget about the teapot, and release all the prisoners. Because you'd know they couldn't all be guilty."

The Captain had just finished talking when there was a sound of excited voices outside and the door flew open and in came all those who had been led out to be executed, headed by Sir Walter, and flung themselves down at the Queen's feet.

"What's this! What's this!" exclaimed the Queen. "What are you doing in here with your heads on? Why haven't my orders been carried out?"

The head guard, who was Georgie in a gold paper hat, came forward and knelt down.

GEORGIE

Your Majesty's orders were perfectly
   clear:
To chop off the head of each prisoner
   here,
But we just couldn't do it. I know that
   we'll rue it,

And your Majesty'll think us most fright-
fully lax,

But the truth of the thing is—we can't
find the axe!

THE QUEEN

You can't find the axe?

GEORGIE

No, your Majesty, no.

We've hunted most everywhere, looked
high and low.

And even the prisoners helped us, because

They said that obeying your Majesty's
laws

Was much more important than keeping
their heads.

But we've looked in the closets, we've
looked under beds,

We've examined all corners and crannies
and cracks,

But, Your Majesty, honest, we can't find
the axe.

THE QUEEN

Well, the teapot is found, and the thief
   has confessed,
So perhaps after all it is all for the best.
But remember, next time that I order
   heads cut off
I mean what I say, and I will not be put
   off
With such reprehensibly, quite indefen-
   sibly
—Yes, I may say even incomprehensibly
Weak and unlikely excuses. Now go,
And take and confine in the dungeons
   below
This piratical captain. And then you
   make tracks,
And go down to the corner and buy a new
   axe.

SIR WALTER

Oh, your Majesty, please; now you've
   pardoned the rest of us,
And since Kidd,—as a poet at least,—is
   the best of us,
Why not carry it through and pardon
   him too?

It would be a most gracious and kind
thing to do.

THE QUEEN

Sir Walter, your thoughtfulness does you
much credit,
But I don't like to take back a thing when
I've said it.
It's the man I condemn, it isn't the poet.
And yet—well, Sir Walter, I feel that I
owe it
To you and to Alice, since tomorrow
you'll wed,
To give Kidd, since you ask it, a chance
for his head.
If he'll find me a rhyme for "seventy,"
I'm
Quite willing to pardon his terrible
crime.

CAPTAIN KIDD

To find a rhyme for "seventy"
You use the letters "f" and "t."

THE QUEEN

You'd better try again.

CAPTAIN KIDD

Or you can say: in heaven tea
Is served at half past ten.

Well, the Queen thought this was pretty awful, but after all, he'd tried hard, and he *had* made a rhyme. So she pardoned him, and promised to have a duplicate of the royal teapot made for his old mother, and the play ended in general rejoicing.

The applause was deafening, and all the actors took several curtain calls, and Mrs. Wiggins took three, and finally had to make a speech.

"Thank you, my friends," she said, "we have done what we could to give you some pleasure. You have been very good—" Here she broke off and said, "My goodness, I can't stop talking poetry!" So she tried again. "I only wanted to mention that we're grateful for your—" Then she stopped again. "Well, anyway," she said quickly, "thanks!"

Chapter 16

The next day was a quiet one on the farm, for the animals weren't used to sitting up late, and they were all pretty sleepy. Along about eleven o'clock Freddy went over to the cow-barn to congratulate Mrs. Wiggins on her acting, but he was met at the door by Mrs. Wogus, who looked rather worried.

"I don't think she wants to see anybody today," said Mrs. Wogus.

"Why, what's the matter?" the pig asked.

"Well, it's that poetry. She can't seem to stop it. Everything she says rhymes."

"Really?" said Freddy. "Well, I don't think there's anything to worry about. It'll wear off, I expect."

"Dear me, I hope so," said the cow. "Poetry's all right in a play, but around the house—"

"Sister, who's that? Is it the cat?" came Mrs. Wiggins' voice from inside, followed by a deep sigh.

"Goodness, she really is doing it, isn't she?" said Freddy. "You know what I bet would cure her? Scaring her. It's probably sort of like the hiccups, and if you give her a good scare, maybe it would go away." He raised his voice. "Can I come in to see you a minute, Mrs. Wiggins?"

"Oh, yes," said Mrs. Wiggins drearily. "I guess," she added.

So Freddy went in. "Now don't talk," he said. "The more you talk the more you'll rhyme, and the worse you'll feel. Let me do the talking. I just wanted to tell you that I've been keeping an eye on the Snedekers this morning, but they don't seem to be packing up. They've only got three days more, though, before the Beans get back, and my guess is they'll try to sneak away without our knowing it. I just want everybody to be ready to do whatever's necessary to stop them. Even if we have to knock them down and sit on them."

"You can count on me and my sisters three," said Mrs. Wiggins.

"You've only got two sisters," said the pig.

"It wouldn't rhyme if I'd said two. I wish you'd tell me what to do."

"H'm," said Freddy. "Well—" He looked at her anxiously a minute and then suddenly he leaped in the air and let out a piercing squeal. Mrs. Wiggins gave a jump and then backed away from him.

"My goodness, Freddy," she said angrily. "That's a fine thing to do! Come to visit a sick friend, and try to scare her to death! I must say—"

"Hey, wait a minute," said the pig. "You aren't talking poetry any more. I cured you! I scared it out of you!"

"Eh?" said Mrs. Wiggins. "Why, so you have, Freddy. Gracious, you're a clever pig." She looked at him gratefully. "I'll do as much for you some time."

"I wouldn't want the poetry scared out of me," said Freddy. "Though right now I'm pretty sick of it, and that's a fact. I had to push that play through too fast. Well, I must go down to the bank. You be ready if the Snedekers try to get away, won't you?"

"I'll be right here," said Mrs. Wiggins.

But nothing happened that day, or the next. It was on the night of the twenty-fourth —the night before the Beans were to come home—that things began happening.

That night the Snedekers went to bed as usual at about half-past eight. In the Bean parlor the teapot still stood on the little table among the tea things. The parlor was getting darker and darker as the sun sank farther and farther below the western horizon, and at last Mr. Webb, who was standing guard that night, couldn't see it any more at all.

"You go on to bed, mother," he said to Mrs. Webb. "I'll take the first watch. Though I don't believe anything will happen tonight."

"Well, this is the last night we'll have to watch," said Mrs. Webb, "so you keep your eyes open. And wake me at midnight."

Mrs. Webb went down behind Washington Crossing the Delaware and climbed into a hammock of her own spinning which she had slung between one of the screw-eyes on the back of the picture and the head of a tack, and was soon sound asleep.

Mr. Webb walked up and down on the top of the frame for a while, but pretty soon he began to get drowsy. So he went and stood upside down on the lower edge. You don't very often see spiders standing upside down, but if you ever do see one, you will know he is doing it so as to keep from falling asleep. For if he begins to drop off to sleep, he will let go his hold, and then he will drop off whatever he is standing on, and that will wake him up again. It won't hurt him either, because spiders are so light that it doesn't hurt them to fall.

Well, Mr. Webb had been on guard for about an hour when he heard someone moving around upstairs. They were moving very quietly, and at first he didn't pay much attention to it. But when it had gone on for ten minutes or so he went up and waked Mrs. Webb.

"Something going on," he said. "I thought I'd better call you."

Mrs. Webb sat up and listened. "Walking back and forth in their stocking feet," she said. "And that's a bureau drawer. They're packing their suitcases. We'd better warn the animals."

"Someone's coming downstairs," said Mr. Webb.

There were stealthy footsteps on the stairs, and then the parlor door opened.

"Be quiet!" whispered Aunt Effie's voice.

"Eh, Effie," said Uncle Snedeker's whisper, "don't see why we can't have a light. Ouch! There, I knew it. Ruined my big toe on that chair, that's what I did."

"Stand still and let me get it then," said Aunt Effie. "We mustn't show a light or the animals will see it and know we're leaving. I hope you've got all your belongings, Snedeker. There'll be no coming back, once we've started. Have you got the key to the car?"

The Webbs didn't wait for any more. Down they went from the picture frame, leg over leg, and through the crack in the baseboard to the little nest of shavings under the floor where Eeny, who was on guard there that night, was fast asleep. They tickled his nose until he woke up, and then they climbed on his back and away they went, under the floor between the beams, and then outdoors through the hole the mice had gnawed, and down toward the pigpen. Across the barnyard they galloped on that historic ride, like two Paul Reveres riding to warn their friends that the enemy were on the move. At the pigpen door Eeny slid to a stop. Mrs. Webb jumped off, and Mr. Webb rode on to warn the other animals.

Five minutes after Eeny had started from the house, the animals had all quietly gathered in the barn, and had then gone to the posts which Freddy and Jinx had assigned them. For the pig and the cat had worked out a plan. It was a good plan. Freddy, in his favorite disguise of a sunbonnet and an old dress of Mrs. Bean's, was to lie down in the driveway just inside the gate. When the Snedekers started to drive away, their headlights would shine on him, and they would stop. Then Freddy, who to all appearances would be an old lady who had fainted away, would moan a few times. The Snedekers couldn't very well drive away and leave her there. After all, they were really pretty kindhearted people. They would have to get out and help her into the house and make her a cup of tea or something. So while they were carrying her into the house the other animals would sneak out, take the suitcases, and hide them somewhere.

The first part of the plan worked all right. The Snedekers came quietly out of the house, put their suitcases in the back seat of the car, then got in, started the engine, and drove quickly down towards the gate. And there was Freddy, looking very old and sick and helpless, lying right in the middle of the drive. The car stopped.

"Eh, Effie," said Uncle Snedeker, "it's an

old woman. Been took sick, likely."

Aunt Effie was already getting out. She knelt down beside Freddy. "Can we help you?" she said.

Freddy gave a heart-rending groan.

"Here, Snedeker," said Aunt Effie. "We must help her into the house. Poor old thing. My goodness, what were you doing out on the road so late at night?"

Uncle Snedeker had got out now, too, but as he leaned down to lift Freddy up, his foot slipped on a pebble, and in trying to get his balance he brushed against the sun-bonnet and knocked it off.

"Clumsy!" said Aunt Effie, and then she saw Freddy's face. "Snedeker!" she exclaimed. "It's that pig! Quick! It's a trick! Get into the car." And before the animals could rush out to stop them, almost before Freddy could roll out of the way, they were back in the car. Uncle Snedeker had stepped on the accelerator, and with a roar they were through the gate and off down the road.

The animals rushed out from their hiding places to gaze disconsolately after them. For

There was Freddy . . . lying right in the middle of the drive.

a few minutes nobody said anything. Their disappointment was too deep for words. Then Robert said:

"Well, there goes the teapot. I don't know how we can look Mrs. Bean in the face to-morrow."

"That plan of yours was just dandy, Freddy," said Charles. "Now if you'd listened to me—"

"Oh, shut up, rooster," said Jinx. "We did the best we knew how. There's no use quarreling about it. We must think how to get the teapot back."

"It'll be in Ohio by morning," said Freddy sadly.

"Before it is day it will be miles away," said Mrs. Wiggins, and then she sighed. "Oh, dear," she said, "the rhyming's come back, with all this excitement."

"Where's Weedly?" said someone suddenly.

"He was with me a few minutes ago," said Jinx. "He was to help me get the suitcases. Wonder where he is?"

"Probably gone to sleep somewhere," said

Charles. "If some animals could just stick to their instructions, and not—"

"You leave Weedly alone," interrupted Jinx.

"Well, where is he, then?"

"It's funny he'd run off like this," said Freddy. "He's been a different pig since he was in that play. So helpful and polite. It isn't like him. Maybe we'd better look for him."

But though they hunted for an hour, Weedly was not to be found.

Chapter 17

The Snedekers' old car bumped and bounced as it followed the glare of its headlights down the road towards Ohio. Uncle Snedeker, with his hat jammed on the back of his head, clung grimly to the steering wheel, and Aunt Effie, sitting bolt upright with her shawl drawn tight about her shoulders, swayed to and fro with the motion. Occasionally, as they went over an extra large bump, her bonnet was snapped over one eye. Then she would straighten it. But she didn't complain, partly

268

because the car made so much noise that Uncle Snedeker couldn't have heard her, and partly because, if she opened her mouth, she was afraid that she would bite her tongue.

After twenty miles or so, however, Uncle Snedeker slowed down a little. "There," he said, "I guess those animals won't overtake us now."

"No," said Aunt Effie. "I guess not. You know, Snedeker, I'm kind of sorry to leave. It was a pleasant life on that farm. And a more mannerly set of animals I've never seen."

"Eh, well," said Uncle Snedeker, "you can't have everything. And you *would* have that teapot, Effie. If it hadn't been for that, I don't say I wouldn't have liked to stay a spell longer myself."

"Yes," said Aunt Effie. "Orenville's going to seem sort of slow, I'm afraid. Without all those pleasant animals around."

"Eh, well, you'll have all your friends."

"That's true. But somehow, Snedeker, when you take them one by one—those friends of ours—well, I'd hate to think that I could prefer a pig to Mrs. Ocumpaugh, or an old horse to Cousin Henry Wells, but—" She broke off. "Well, anyway," she said, "we've got the teapot." And she turned around to give a triumphant look at the suitcases in the back seat. And suddenly gave a loud cry. For the suitcases weren't there!

Uncle Snedeker put the brake on so hard that Aunt Effie's nose was nearly flattened against the windshield. They both climbed out, and then they searched the car from bumper to bumper. But the suitcases were gone.

"Snedeker," said Aunt Effie, "you ought to be drawn and quartered. You left them behind."

"But I didn't," protested Uncle Snedeker. "I put 'em in—honest I did."

"You couldn't have. You left 'em on the barn floor. Well, there's no use arguing. Get in. We must go back."

So back they went. Most of the animals had gone off gloomily to bed by the time they drove into the barnyard, but Jinx was still wandering about, looking in the most unlikely places for the vanished Weedly. Freddy too was up. The failure of his plan had been a hard blow. He was a thoroughly desperate and discouraged pig, and how he was ever to face the Beans on their return in the morning he didn't know. He was sitting disconsolately on the edge of the porch, wondering if it wouldn't perhaps be better for him to disappear and never be seen again, when the Snedekers drove in.

The car went into the barn, and after watching for a few minutes while the Snedekers hunted for the suitcases, Jinx and Freddy went in.

"Something wrong, ma'am?" Freddy asked innocently.

"Go away, pig," said Aunt Effie crossly. "A fine friend you are!"

"Why, I told you we'd do everything we could to keep you from getting the teapot," said Freddy. "But you got it anyway. So we're the ones that ought to be mad."

"Got it, eh?" said Uncle Snedeker. "Yes, we did like fun!" Then he stopped suddenly. "Eh, Effie," he said doubtfully, "maybe I hadn't ought to have said anything."

"It can't do any harm to tell 'em," said Aunt Effie. "I guess they know it. The suitcases aren't here." She turned to Freddy. "You animals better hand over those suitcases if you know what's good for you," she said threateningly.

"The suitcases!" said Freddy. "Why—we haven't got the suitcases. What are you talking about?"

"We left them here, and they aren't here now," said Aunt Effie. "Come; hand 'em over."

Freddy and Jinx looked at her in bewilderment. "Why, honestly, ma'am," said Jinx, "we haven't got them."

Aunt Effie sat down on the running board of the car. "Freddy," she said solemnly, "I've always thought you were a pretty honest pig. You tried to fool us into thinking you were a sick old lady, but I guess that was fair. Anyway, you've never told a lie to me. Are you telling the truth?"

"I suppose I ought to get mad at you, ma'am, for doubting my word," said Freddy. "But if the suitcases are really gone— Well, now, if we *did* have them, we'd have taken the teapot out and hidden it in a safe place where you couldn't find it, wouldn't we?"

"I expect you would," said Aunt Effie.

"And in that case, we wouldn't need to lie to you, would we? We could just tell you so. There are hundreds of places on this farm where we could hide such a thing, and you'd never find it in the wide world. So why should you think we are lying to you now?"

"H'm," said Aunt Effie. "Yes, that makes sense. I beg your pardon, Freddy. And yours, Jinx. But the fact is the suitcases are gone." She got up suddenly. "Snedeker," she said, "take a lantern and look down the road. Better take a club with you, for if you find 'em these animals will try to take them away from you."

"We certainly will," said Freddy.

"Good," said Aunt Effie. "I like honesty, even in an enemy. I'll go search the house. I don't know what good it'll do, but they must be somewhere."

"Get the rest of the animals up, Jinx," said Freddy when the Snedekers had started on their hunt. "We must hunt too. It beats me what can have happened to the suitcases, but we've as good a chance of finding them as the Snedekers, since nobody knows where they are. Anyway, it's our only chance."

So all night long the hunt went on, up and down the road and through house and barn. But when the sun finally came up and looked over the hill at them, the suitcases were still missing. And so, too, was Little Weedly.

After breakfast the Snedekers gave up the search for a while. They had been up all night, and they lay down to take a nap. The Beans were due on the nine o'clock train, and at eight the animals helped Hank to get hitched up to the phaeton and he drove off to Centerboro to meet them. After some hesitation, Freddy went along, to explain to them before they got home how matters stood at the farm.

Just before ten o'clock the animals began to gather at the gate to welcome the returning travelers. Pretty soon they heard in the distance the clop-clop of Hank's hoofs, and then up the road came the phaeton. The animals

At eight the animals helped Hank to get hitched.

set up a cheer as it drew up at the gate. Then out they got—Mrs. Bean in a new Paris hat, and the two adopted boys, Byram and Adoniram, and last, Mr. Bean, looking very spruce and foreign in a new cutaway coat and striped trousers.

Mrs. Bean rushed about hugging one animal after another. "My land," she said, "it's good to be back!" Mr. Bean just stood still and puffed on his pipe until the sparks flew and his head was almost invisible through the smoke. You could see that he was almost bursting with pride and happiness. "Bon jour, animals. Bon jour," he kept saying. "That's French for 'howdedo'," he explained.

"Mr. Bean's got quite Frenchified during his stay in Paris," said Mrs. Bean. "But never mind that now. There's one thing I want to say to you animals. Freddy has been telling me about the goings-on while we've been away, and I want to say right now: don't you worry one mite about that old teapot. If it's gone it's gone, and that's the end of it, and we don't care one bit—not one particle. Do we, Mr. B?"

"Glad to get rid of it," said Mr. Bean. "Oui, oui."

"And," went on Mrs. Bean, "we think you animals have been just wonderful, and we've got presents for every one of you, and as soon as we get our things unpacked— Oh," she said suddenly, "there's your aunt, Mr. B." For the Snedekers had come out on the porch.

Mr. Bean went toward his aunt. "Bon jour, Aunt Effie," he said.

"Good morning, William," said Aunt Effie. She faced him with stiff dignity. "I don't know as you'll want to shake hands with me when you've heard just why we're here."

"Heard all about it," said Mr. Bean gruffly. "Tried to get the teapot again. But tryin' and doin's two different things." He held out his hand, and as Aunt Effie slowly put hers into it, he bent and kissed it. "Enchanté, madame," he said. "That means," he said, "I'm glad to see you. Got anything to eat in the house?"

But Aunt Effie was staring at him in complete amazement. "William Bean," she said, "maybe you're a-laughing behind those whiskers. Nobody'll ever know. But laughing or not, I'll tell you I never in all my life expected to see the time when anybody'd kiss my hand with such real fine foreign manners, and if I'd hunted from now till Doomsday I'd never have picked anybody more unlikely to do it than you."

"Sorry you don't like it, Aunt Effie," said Mrs. Bean. "Mr. B. was so impressed with the manners of those French people that he tries 'em out every now and then. Just in the family, of course."

"Don't like it!" said Aunt Effie. "Of course I like it. I just didn't think he had it in him, that's all. Snedeker!" she said suddenly. "Let's see you try it." And she held out her hand.

Uncle Snedeker blushed. "Aw, Effie," he said protestingly.

"Come on," said Aunt Effie firmly. "You aren't going to be outdone— My land!" she said in a horrified whisper. "Look!"

Through the gate limped little Weedly. He was covered with dirt and scratches, but in his mouth he carried the silver teapot.

The animals, who had already been amazed

by the unexpected courtliness of Mr. Bean's imported manners, were now completely stupefied. They crowded round as Weedly walked slowly up and put the teapot down in front of Mrs. Bean.

"Weedly!" exclaimed Jinx. "Where did you get it?" He turned to Mrs. Bean. "This is Freddy's cousin, Weedly, Mrs. Bean," he said. "He's my adopted nephew."

"How do you do, Weedly," said Mrs. Bean. "My land, where did you find the teapot?"

"Well, ma'am," said Weedly, "you see, when Freddy was pretending to be a sick old lady, the Snedekers got out of their car. We were supposed to wait until they carried Freddy into the house, but I guess I got a little impatient, and maybe I hadn't ought to have done it, but I climbed right in to get the suitcases. And then they saw it was Freddy and jumped in the car and drove off. So I just sort of scrooched down in the back seat, and after they'd gone a mile or two and weren't looking back any more, I threw the suitcases out and jumped after them."

"Good piece of work," grumbled Mr.

Bean, and that from him was a pretty fine compliment, for he wasn't one to praise people much to their faces.

"Well," said Weedly, "I guess it was lucky it was an open car. Anyway, I opened the suitcases and found the teapot, and I'd been back before with it, only when I jumped, I twisted my ankle, and I couldn't walk very fast."

"Land sakes," said Mrs. Bean, kneeling down beside him. "Let me see it. You come right in the house and let me bandage it up, and get you something good to eat. My, you're a brave pig."

"He's *my* nephew," said Jinx proudly.

"Just a minute," said Aunt Effie. She stood very stiff and straight and looked sternly at Weedly. "Kindly bring that teapot to me."

Weedly looked doubtfully at Mrs. Bean, but she nodded assent, and he picked up the teapot and put it in Aunt Effie's hand.

Aunt Effie looked at it for a moment, then she said: "William, I came here to get this teapot, because I have a right to it. No," she went on quickly, as he began puffing furiously at his pipe, preparatory to bursting into speech, "you needn't turn yourself into a volcano. You can blow your head off, but I'm going to say my say. Well, I've got the teapot. But while I've been here, I've learned some things. I've learned to admire these animals for their fine manners, and to respect them for their bravery. They've fought me hard and honestly, and at the same time we've been friends. I think I'm right in saying that, Freddy?"

"You are, ma'am," said the pig.

"Well, I'd like to stay friends. I'd rather have friends than a silver teapot. Here," she said, suddenly thrusting it towards Mrs. Bean. "It's yours. Keep it."

"Three cheers for Aunt Effie!" shouted Robert. But while the animals were cheering, Mr. Bean turned and went to the phaeton and dragged out a square box. He hastily unwrapped and opened it, and took out another silver teapot of about the same size, but with a different design.

"See here," he said. "I got this teapot in London for Mrs. Bean. Took her fancy in a store window, so I bought it. Man said it belonged to Queen Elizabeth. That ain't likely, but it's right pretty anyhow. Well, we ain't any use for two teapots, have we, Mrs. B.?"

"Good grief, I should say not!" said Mrs. Bean, smiling. "One of 'em's enough to keep polished and bright."

"Well, then," said Mr. Bean, "give Aunt Effie her old teapot, and for land's sake let's go in the house and unpack the presents for the animals."

Usually when Mr. Bean said to do something, everybody did it at once. But this time nobody moved. For all of them—animals and humans—were looking at Aunt Effie. Even Uncle Snedeker was staring, and under his breath he said: "Well, set fire to my coat tails!" And well he might exclaim, for two large tears were rolling down over Aunt Effie's cheeks.

Suddenly she caught Uncle Snedeker by the hand. "Come," she said sharply. "We can't stand here all day. We must get back home." And she started to drag him out to their car.

But Mrs. Bean nudged Mr. Bean, and he

got quickly in front of Aunt Effie and bowed very low. "Madam," he said, "we beg you to accept our hospitality for as long as you care to stay." Then as Aunt Effie hesitated, he dropped on one knee. "S'il-vous-plait," he said in French, and kissed her hand.

And Aunt Effie burst into a loud laugh and kissed him on the cheek, and they all went into the house, Mr. Bean carrying Weedly in his arms.

"So that was *really* Queen Elizabeth's teapot," said Mrs. Wiggins.

"And if you were really Queen Elizabeth," said Freddy, "you'd have drunk your tea out of it."

"But I wouldn't be here now," said Mrs. Wiggins. "I'd rather be a cow. Oh, dear," she said, "Every time I get a little excited the rhyming comes on again. I guess I'd better go lie down." And she walked slowly off towards the cowbarn. But the other animals sat down in a ring around the back door to wait for their presents.

Dear Libary

sorry

I cannot

on the

Book

the